FAITH BALDWIN

Face Toward the Spring

ILLUSTRATED BY ADRIANNE BLAIR

One of America's most beloved writers, in this heart-warming book, reveals the kernel of her philosophy — a personal vision of life which has given her strength and solace through times of trial and sorrow. Like Anne Morrow Lindbergh in "Gift From the Sea," Miss Baldwin evokes from every woman reader an immediate response.

FACE TOWARD THE SPRING is an intimate and inspirational journey through the seasons — one woman's thoughts, hopes, fears and joys, written with honesty, clarity and courage. In these pages, Miss Baldwin is concerned with communication in human relationships and with God; blossoms, brides, and bliz-

(continued on back flap)

Books by Faith Baldwin

Three Women
Departing Wings
Alimony
The Office-Wife
The Incredible Year
Make-Believe
Today's Virtue
Skyscraper
Week-end Marriage
District Nurse
Self-made Woman
Beauty
White-Collar Girl
Love's a Puzzle
Innocent Bystander
Wife versus Secretary
Within a Year
Honor Bound
American Family
The Puritan Strain
The Moon's Our Home
Private Duty
The Girls of Divine Corners
Men Are Such Fools!
That Man Is Mine
The Heart Has Wings
Twenty-four Hours a Day
Manhattan Nights
Enchanted Oasis
Rich Girl, Poor Girl
Hotel Hostess
The High Road
Career by Proxy
White Magic
Station Wagon Set
Rehearsal for Love
"Something Special"
Letty and the Law
Medical Center
And New Stars Burn
Temporary Address: Reno
The Heart Remembers
Blue Horizons
Breath of Life
Five Women in Three Novels
The Rest of My Life with You
Washington, U.S.A.
You Can't Escape
He Married a Doctor
Change of Heart
Arizona Star
A Job for Jenny
No Private Heaven
Woman on Her Way
Sleeping Beauty
Give Love the Air
Marry for Money
They Who Love
The Golden Shoestring
Look Out for Liza
The Whole Armor
The Juniper Tree
Face Toward the Spring

POETRY

Sign Posts
Widow's Walk

Face Toward the Spring

By FAITH BALDWIN

WITH ILLUSTRATIONS BY ADRIANNE BLAIR

Rinehart & Company, Inc. *New York Toronto*

Published simultaneously in Canada by
Clarke, Irwin & Company, Ltd., Toronto

Printed in the United States of America

Library of Congress Catalog Card Number: 56-9939

In Dedication

Derin muhabbet ve shükrânla
hâtifî mürshidim Mustafaya

who taught me that all men are truly brothers
and that each finds his own way to God.

A Grateful Acknowledgment

To the editors of the *Christian Herald*, who, some years ago, opened the pages of their magazine to me;
to Stewart Richardson, of Rinehart and Company, whose encouragement and patient editing made this book possible;
and to Madame Meliha Zafir, of Istanbul, who translated into Modern Turkish a part of the dedication.

FAITH BALDWIN

Foreword

During a year's time the average woman, preoccupied with the ordinary duties, and the small or large crises that arise in every family, often remarks that she "doesn't have time to think."

She does. The thinking process, the stream of consciousness, goes on about its own business whether or not she is aware of it. But consciousness operates upon several levels.

Long ago I wrote a short article for the *Christian Herald* at the request of the editor in chief, Dr. Daniel A. Poling. It was to commemorate Father's Day and I think it was called "I Wind My Father's Watch."

Later I wrote still another article, and finally, because the editors had probably decided to live dangerously, I found myself doing six a year, for a specific purpose.

One year, for personal reasons, there were only five.

In these articles I was thinking aloud and as I went on I found the level of my consciousness changing. This was due somewhat to the fact that I had become accustomed to writing in what, foı me, was a new field, as with few exceptions my work had been fiction. But it was mainly because since the first month of 1954 I had come into a different way of thought . . . with, for my own purposes at least, a better grasp of why I was thinking in such a way and also with the hope that there would be, here and there, a reader who could say from her own experience that she, too, had thought, believed, and pondered upon certain things.

The professional writer is not greatly different from other men or women (though sometimes he thinks he is). The only difference is the ability to express himself, on paper. No personal merit or credit accrues to this ability; he has not, himself, created it. The only possible merit lies in what he does with it and to what extent he is self-disciplined in hard work.

The final reward is the reader—even if there be only one—who shares with the writer: who feels, understands, and perhaps, through a sentence reaches out and goes beyond the thought expressed, and so finds a new horizon.

What is here set down is not all of her who wrote it; but a part only, for there is much that is inexpressible over a year's time; and to pin the butterfly wing of the valid emotion to paper with the key of a typewriter is usually to destroy it. And, as I have said elsewhere, all communication, except the communication of the human spirit with its Creator, is imperfect, whether by speech or by the written word.

Foreword

There are thoughts and reachings-out that are not compatible with magazine policies, which are even incompatible with the policies of publishers. And there are also the intangibles and imponderables.

As a man thinketh, so is he—for we are only what we think. Sometimes we think we are thinking, yet are not; sometimes we feel we do not think at all, but do. The unspoken, the unwritten, the unformulated, all these are part of the maturing process that goes on within us as long as we live in this world—and, I believe, hereafter.

Let us say, then, that in these few pages are printed a part of what one average woman *knows* she has thought in the brief span of a year.

Contents

❀ *Face Toward the Spring*

NOVEMBER

I. ❀ *Face Toward the Spring*

As I sit at my desk and look out the window, I see a bleak November landscape swept with the cold winds which are the advance guards of winter. Last night's rain has frozen and the icicles are already making shining daggers at the eaves. The storm windows are on and my room is heavy with the warmth of steam heat. My winter clothes smell of moth balls, the woodbox is full, I have my winter's reading in the library; in every way I am ready for the cold season. And yet I find myself thinking of spring. Again I turn to look out the window and, although I see November, I think of March.

March is a month many people dislike. In my New England it is a temperamental month, blowing hot and cold by turns. I have known March days when a light jacket was too warm—and a heavy fur coat was not warm enough. A New England March can produce almost any kind of weather—rain, sunshine, snow, or summer heat. And often—fickle as an adolescent girl—it can switch from one extreme to another without turning a March hare.

I don't like wind and sleet. And I can't adjust to abrupt weather changes. Yet I have come to like March. It is an in-between time. It comes after the heavy storms and the heart-shaped gaiety of St. Valentine's Day. And usually it comes before Easter—although sometimes it brings Easter to us before its close. Also I have a sentimental attachment for March. It is the month in which my older son was born—at a time when winter left the frozen snow banked high in the city streets.

Now—before winter's first heavy snowfall, and aware of the many snowfalls to come before March comes howling in; before the Christmas carols sing out from our church and invade the frosty air with their sweetness and cheer—I think of March and spring before winter has actually closed in, and I have a curious sort of hope. Why? Because I *can* write of spring while winter is yet here.

In March the birds begin to return. Where I live the fox sparrow will make his short, rufous appearance. The winter birds, which I have fed every day, will not as yet have gone. Each morning I will listen for their spring song—and at the first familiar note I will reach for my binoculars or cast an eager glance out toward the birdbath to see what new visitor is there.

After March comes April, and—this year—Easter. But it is not necessary to look that far ahead. March is enough, for the first signs of spring—the tiny green shoots—will appear and, to eyes grown weary of winter, even the lowly skunk cabbage will look beautiful. Under the heavy mantle of snow the wondrous eternal growth will begin to stir. The sap, released from frosty dreams, will run freely in the still bare-bough trees. And once again winter-locked hearts will awaken.

I suppose that one of life's wonders is that capacity of human beings to look forward to something. The soul that has ceased to look ahead is desolate indeed, sealed in a perpetual winter.

I love to live in a part of the country where there are four definite seasons. This is not to say that, in our changeable climate, summer does not occasionally invade spring or autumn. Or that winter does not often come long before the calendar says it's winter. But on the average we have four distinct seasons—with none so enduring that you grow bored with it, none so firmly established that you feel there is nothing to look forward to.

And so it is, before winter's actual beginning, with the temperature below twenty and a cold wind whispering of snow, that I dream of March and the awakening of my small portion of earth. In other parts of the country March will bring more than the promise of spring—it will bring the flowers and the earth-warming sun. For years I have dreamed of following the sun—of starting in the deep South and coming north with spring, of seeing spring wherever I go.

Here, in March, I bundle up against the sudden cold and the slowly falling snow. Or a calm, sunny day I unwrap myself and go into the woods to see if anything has awakened. Standing by the brook—with its early-morning patina of ice—I hear the fresh, clean, cold water rushing past augmented by heavy rains or by melted snow from far away. The trees stand bare, yet if I were to put my ear against a bough I know I would hear life speaking; in this month the small animals come out from hiding and the birds, resident and transient, begin rehearsing their spring song. To awaken in the morning and hear that music is to come alive again.

This spring must have a special meaning for me, because the climate of the heart is not always that of the weather. I was still aware of the numbing depths of an earlier winter that was darker and more desolate than any I had ever known. The reading of a thermometer, the date on a newspaper, the calendar itself, was of no moment. In summer's most torrid heat, I froze. Winter seemed the true climate of my heart.

But here is a lesson we must all learn, no matter how self-engrossed we may be. The earth turns, the sun wheels overhead, the months parade by, and the seasons change. The deepest winter has its frosty face turned toward spring, and so too must the heart lean springward. As has been said all too often, life goes on. And, as on earth, so too does it go on in that other world. To disbelieve this is to disbelieve everything we see all about us. For March and the coming of spring is the fulfillment of a promise. On earth we pass from winter into springtime—and beyond the earth it must always be spring.

In the routine of everyday life, most of us look forward to spring without realizing it. We stoke our furnaces, build our hearth fires, and check our storm windows, and slip housewifely away, yet we think ahead to the day when the fires will die out and the storm windows and doors come off. And we say, "Soon it will be spring."

But there are matters which go beyond the reorganizing of a house—matters of the spirit, which now begins to free itself from its winter bindings. Here too a housecleaning is possible, with storm windows removed to let the sunshine enter on waves of sweet clean air which reach into every dark corner of the lonely heart.

Nothing is static. The seasons do not remain fixed nor even mark time. Always there is a new beginning. There is no time of the year when there is not something to look forward to. And while the despairing heart may often feel that this is true of the seasons but not of life itself, there is—however much one may deny it—always the hope of the future.

Nothing is more wonderful in our lives than the fact that tomorrow never comes. If it did, it would mean an ending. Always, when we go to sleep at night, we think, "There is tomorrow." Yet when we awaken, it is today—tomorrow is still to be. For all of us, however unhappy we may find ourselves, there is a future—although never do we know what shape it will take. It may be another person's need or someone else's happiness. It may be a new and exciting interest of which yesterday we would never have dreamed. It may be a new way of serving our friends. Whatever it is, it is in the tomorrow that will become today, the yesterday that is still now.

And so I think ahead to March, as a new start, a new future. Without spring, life would perish. And without the assurance of a future, on this earth and beyond it, so, too, would our spirit perish. And often we have seen it die—for we have all known those who are manacled to the past, existing barely in the present, and moving through a futureless existence.

Open your hearts now to the vibrant winds of

March. Feel the warm sun even as you watch the feathery snow fall. Listen to the bird song, valiant and clear, however chilling the winds may be. And see through the bare branch the promise of the leaf. For no matter how often it may again intrude on us, with the promise of March we turn our backs on winter and face toward the spring—a spring in which once again we are privileged to see the promise of eternal life.

2. ꕥ *In the Fullness of Time*

Writing in the midst of a busy season—and what season isn't busy?—I think about the increasing tensions and pressures in our world, and in our bodies, minds, and spirits. It seems to me that never has our haste, hurry, and impatience been as marked as it is now. I sometimes feel that we are like sheep rushing headlong off the edge of a cliff into some bottomless abyss.

I know few really relaxed people. Some who appear calm on the outside are not really so inwardly. Nor do people seem to have time for each other. "Think I'll go visiting," the elder ladies of my youth would say. Then they'd put on their bonnets, sally forth, and come back looking refreshed and stimulated. Nowadays people will drop in, saying, "I can't stay a moment." Or a young woman will come for tea—and halfway through the second cup she will suddenly fly out the front door because she has to be at home for a telephone call, or has to catch a train, or must go to a meeting. As my grandmother used to say, she hardly warms the seat of her chair before she's off, calling back over her shoulder, "I'll be seeing you." And then she doesn't, for months thereafter.

Often when I meet people on the street, they call out "How are you?" and then dash off, leaving me wondering if they really care how I am or if they are even aware that they've asked.

But then I'm not relaxed either. And, although I have read at least a dozen how-to-do-it books, this business of deliberately relaxing one's muscles from scalp to toes eludes me—to say nothing of sitting like a rag doll, limp as a dishcloth, and blanking out one's mind. My mind wanders. I keep thinking that the curtains need to be cleaned or that I forgot to order the fish.

Latterly I have tried to take stock of myself. After all, I am the person I know best (and also probably the least)—the person I have to live with day in and day out—the one human being from whom I cannot escape. I can flee to the ends of the earth (and actually have on a few occasions), but I have to take myself along—which is sometimes discouraging. And I know quite well that my tempo, always a fast one, has been stepped up instead of slowed down, as it certainly should be at my age. Now I find myself hounded by an enormous sense of urgency. Surely, none of us was born with this nagging at the base of our minds. Perhaps it develops as we grow older, according to the time and circumstances in which we live. Sometimes I frighten myself with my feeling of impatience. It isn't with people (although sometimes with their attitudes); it is more often with events. Whenever I want something I want it now, immediately—which is extremely childish. Always there is the I-can't-wait feeling about it. Even just shopping. Many people I know shop carefully, thoughtfully, as if doing comparison shopping. And they do it not only with merchandise but also with other things—marriage, education, even creeds. But not me. I have to run right out and get what I want. As a result I am often disappointed, disturbed, even disdainful when I contemplate what I have selected. And I have to pay for it.

It is not so important with just merchandise. But there are vital things we rush out to get which cannot be returned, but for which we still have to pay. Friendship, for instance. How often we rush headlong into friendship only to find that it does not measure up to our standards. But by then we are committed. We just can't say to someone, "I find you a different person from the one I thought you were; so I am herewith returning your friendship."

Very often we rush into responsibility, taking on

something in our eagerness to proclaim ourselves capable and strong enough to do the job—only to find we have neither the ability nor the strength. I thought of this after, in a glow of pleasure, I had accepted a position on the board of my most beloved charity. I sat back and wondered. How much could I really contribute? It's one thing to sponsor a charity, make speeches, or write publicity pieces, but quite another to work dependably, with patience and vision, in an executive capacity.

In troubled times many people gallop into matrimony. Love, of course, is unpredictable. You may fall in love within an eye's twinkling—and out again as fast. Or else you fall in love, you hope, forever. If you are fortunate, it *is* forever. Or perhaps it is a slow development rather than a sudden emotional discovery. But particularly during wars, young people are likely to say *I do*, first, and wonder afterward.

Advice doesn't help. If they are blessed, they learn after the adjustment that they were right in the first place. The not-so-fortunate ones discover that they were wrong, and then set out to remedy the situation.

The common attitude seems to be always "I think this is an enduring emotion—but if it isn't, I can get out of it." Which leads me to believe that many don't really intend it to last. They go aboard thinking, "If my marriage sinks, there's always the escape hatch."

The marriages that last are those which are undertaken with the firm intention that they will endure. Not all do, of course. But I never knew a girl—thinking privately that if her marriage didn't "fit" she could, so to speak, always return it to the shop—who had an enduring or happy marriage.

I have been watching the seasons swing. Nature is never in a hurry. She stages storms, floods, hurricanes—and sometimes we feel she is acting according to a sudden whim. But actually it is all slowly building up somewhere far beyond our ken. Sometimes she seems to precipitate us from winter into spring or from autumn into winter without letting us catch our breath. But in reality, beyond the small deviations, the cycle is much the same: a slow, steady growth, a slipping from season into season in an orderly way. Even a sudden early burst of bloom or an unexpected snowstorm does not mean that the process was hurried: the plant was ready; the snow was forming; and, when the time came, there was the bloom . . . the falling snow.

Latterly I have been trying to slow myself up to some extent. I haven't succeeded too well, but I should at least get "E" for effort. At night when I lie awake thinking of all the things I've left undone that day, I endeavor to remind myself that none is worth losing sleep over. And, also, tomorrow is another day.

I suspect that the key is right there in my hand. For tomorrow *is* another day.

For the past two years I have managed, whatever

happened, to take time out for myself. Sometimes it is fifteen minutes, or an hour or longer. I do not spend the time tensely ordering myself to relax, nor do I try to blank out my "grasshopper" mind. I just pray. And because my life is words—such as those I now write—I speak aloud. It is the only way I know to concentrate. This is my form of prayer—talking directly, from the heart and the spirit, to the One who never fails to hear.

After such moments I can leave my room, relaxed, all tension gone, and feeling a refreshment and a serenity that stay with me all the rest of the day. And when I go to bed, I speak again, briefly, in gratitude; and once more when I open my eyes in the morning.

This is not the kneeling praying of my childhood. Nor does it include, except perhaps at the very beginning, any of the prayers we learned in our infancy. It is just talking aloud—and mostly about other people, asking for healing for them, for help, for guidance.

It has worked for me—as other methods work for other people.

I know that I must slow down, for reasons having nothing whatever to do with physical health. Of course such a slowdown is an aid to an overworked heart or a soaring blood pressure. It is also a help against rapid aging. But I think of it as a spiritual remedy. For, although we live in the body, we are anchored in the spirit.

I have never been a faddist. I don't run about practicing odd postures or strange deep-breathing exercises. In my girlhood I used to; I would read books and promptly try to follow their instructions. I never got very far. It wasn't for me. I might say, however, that if I had not been impatient even then, I might have achieved the promised results. But apparently I was not willing to spend months learning one exercise. I wanted to conquer the method instantly.

I believe that everyone must learn to discipline his own drive. It is like having a team of horses—either you drive them—or they drive you. If you give them their heads, you find yourself with runaways on your hands—and runaways can carry you to disaster.

I remember a woman I knew and loved in Germany, long ago. We called her *Grossmutter*. I often used to go to her sunny apartment for lunch or coffee. She had a houseful of old-fashioned furniture, rows and rows of plants, and a fabulous maid who gave us miraculous meals. And after every one of them *Grossmutter* would retire to a stiff sort of chaise longue in the middle of the parlor; she would lie down, close her eyes, put a large white handkerchief over her face, and go to sleep for exactly twenty minutes. It didn't matter who was in the room or if we went on talking—which we did. At the end of the twenty minutes she would remove the handkerchief, sit up, and briskly demand to be caught up on all that had been said while she slept. She must have been close to eighty, perhaps more, when I knew her, and she was strong and vital. She had a simple and firmly rooted faith. She was a happy woman.

I described *Grossmutter* to a friend in Chicago, who is a charming woman, immersed in the antics of her grandchildren and in continual correspondence with her relatives. I don't know how anyone can have so many relatives. Yet she keeps up with them all. She looked at me in surprise and said, "I've always managed to rest every day, no matter where I am—at home, in a hotel, in a car, a plane or a train. I do it at least once a day." And her conscious relaxation showed. For she is a busy woman who doesn't look her age by a dozen years or more.

A little stock taking is always a wise move. The younger you are when you start setting aside a little time for thinking, and not just doing—for getting acquainted with yourself, for opening your receptive spirit to the quiet word of God—the happier you will be in later years. But it's better late than never.

I often sit in a little old rocker in my bedroom and look out the windows at whatever presents itself: trees, in whatever seasonal garb nature has dressed them; the birdbath, sometimes frozen; and always the birds, winter and summer. Sometimes I see the rising sun or a glorious sunset. I look out with my physical eyes, but with my spiritual eyes I am looking within. Often I don't like what I see inside. But that is something I can always talk to God about.

My most favorite hymn, and I have many favorites, is "Dear Lord and Father of Mankind." It expresses in unusually lovely words and melody exactly what I try to achieve, the quiet, the peace, the letting go of tension, the cooling of the fever of living.

Perhaps as we grow older our sense of urgency increases because we think, if only subconsciously, that our time is short, that we must make the most of what is left. But this is only a superficial measurement, for time is not short nor is life brief . . . and making the most of it is not necessarily making the best of it.

The drive increases with spring, when there is so much to do, to see, to be accomplished. Even so, we should slow down. Today's unwritten letter will get written tomorrow. And this isn't a *mañana* philosophy of procrastination. It is a philosophy of first things first. It is more important to rest awhile and contemplate your soul than to make a telephone call or write a letter when neither is vital.

There is no need to hurry. We have Eternity. Sometimes I hear people say, half in despair and always with incredulity, "Well, I suppose life could go on without me." Life will always go on, but it will not go on "without" anyone, for life, in God, is everlasting and all we need to know about it is that God lives—and so do we, going from strength to strength.

These are the things you come to know when you learn to control your drive, to curb your urgency and impatience, when you take the time to forget about time and to sit awhile by yourself and talk quietly with your Creator.

DECEMBER

I. ❀ *This Is Promise*

December—any December—is unpredictable. We do not know, in our New England climate, at least, if it will be fair or stormy. We cannot anticipate how much snow will fall, but this we do know—that the trees will be bare against the sky, black branch and trunk like a Chinese etching.

We have planted alders, the black ones that bear red berries. But this past summer afflicted them with a blight. But never mind, I say to myself, they will be all right again; they will recover. On the little pond a skim of ice, and it will not be long before the mallards find it. They nest early—in February, I think.

The pond is never frozen solid, since it is brook-fed and there is always a bubble of fresh-running water.

Now the winter transient birds come. You may awaken any morning to a strange small chorus of them and see new diners at the feeders. We have purple finches nesting all summer long and singing fit to burst their throats. But I have not forgotten last year's cardinal on December twenty-first nor last year's bluebird sitting on top of a pheasant shelter eight days thereafter.

This is a place of magic; from my window I look out and see something strange and something familiar, both welcome. Last summer I came quite close to a great blue heron. I could see him without binoculars. I have seen the small green heron closer still. Both posed majestically at the pond's edge.

Now is the season of winter sunsets—the apple green, clear and cold, the great sweeping scarlets and gold, the dusky mauves and rose. I run from window to window, from the west panes where the light is like that of another world—and, for all I know, may be—to the south and east; yes, even the north, flushed and enchanting in the afterglow. No leaves obscure the colors. Straight down from heaven they pour through the naked branches, like oil upon the pond. They warm the snow; they look like tattered banners flying. Now and again on autumn and winter nights we see the mysterious splendor of the northern lights. The first time I saw these was during

World War I, on a country road on Long Island. I got out of the car and stood spellbound, not knowing and afraid. In later years I saw them often on the St. Lawrence River and never ceased to marvel.

In this season the rabbit and the fox and the slender weasel sleep. The woodchuck that came to sit under an apple tree all summer and turn an apple in his little black hands also is sleeping. It is the time for the hibernation of animals. But in the house it is time for the vast excitement, communicable without words, of the Christmas season. Even with the children grown and gone.

You'd think that after over fifty Christmases I would weary of the little traditional home things, the trimmings, so to speak. If not weary, at least feel the keen edge blunted against the hard shape of so many years. This is not so. I begin to grow excited in August; by September I am making lists; by October I am knee-deep in Christmas preparations. This has nothing to do with the brutal fact that nowadays because of rushed printers I am asked to write my Christmas cards in June, or at the latest in July!

All the past Christmases, which are between me and the children, are like a strong invisible chain, binding yet not impeding. In Chicago, the eldest born will think of his childhood, and his wife recall her first Christmas under his mother's roof. In Nashville, the older daughter will fill the little stockings of two girl babies and recall her own stocking hung by our mantelpiece. Perhaps one of the twins will be with us, here. But wherever they are, they will remember.

This is the gay and lighter face of this sacred season. The other face, two faces on a pure gold coin, is solemn and thrilling. It is promise and hope—the hope of all the world. It is the salvation and glory that have endured for nearly two thousand years.

I write, of course, before Christmas, but I write myself *into* Christmas. The rain I hear as I sit beneath the lamplight is not rain but the soft purr of falling snow. The stars are this night obscured, but I can see them in this coming December. For December is a month of stars.

Believe me, it is easy to project oneself into Christmas—on the grayest, saddest November day, in an apple orchard in the rose-white spring, or looking out on blazing August skies. For Christmas is twelve months of the year. It is always with us—the promise, the hope, the salvation, the wonder, and the glory. Christ is born every day, in every month in every year, in any heart which turns to Him in praise, in thanksgiving, and in love.

Now the rain comes down harder. It is like drumbeats and the wind blows, but I am lost in a dream of snow and stars. For the Christmas Star is a shining hope, a silver flame which cannot be quenched; not by sorrow or distrust, never by war or rumor of war. This is the month of stars—the month of the Promised Star, which will never fail us who seek it, who experience the healing light.

Christmas is not happy for everyone. There are those who are alone, who have been alone for a long time, and those recently left lonely. There are those who suffer great pain in their own persons or feel the knife turn in another's wound. There are those who are disillusioned, who are in desperate straits, who are confined, beaten, knowing injustice, knowing terror by day and night. There are miserable people all over the world and people who have lost everything they own—even hope. Yet, for them, too, the Star shines, if they but look for it.

And so, God bless you, and for all a blessed Christmastide.

2. *Many Mansions*

Once, when I returned from a fourteen-week trip around the world, I found myself in a vortex of family excitement and welcoming festivities. On the less carefree side were mountains of mail and social and business obligations. For a long time these problems had seemed very remote. I knew they all existed—but I was so far away! Distance may lend enchantment, but it also breeds carelessness. At ten thousand miles you think, "What can I possibly do about it?"

And then suddenly you are home and there are the problems waiting for you.

Ever since I've been home, friends, and even strangers, in letters or in person, have besieged me with the same request—"Tell me all about your trip." This would be impossible, unless I were to write a small book—which I have no intention of doing. Yet little by little I find myself recalling highlights of my trip—the amusing things that happened, my pleasure in visiting old friends and familiar places, the excitement of meeting new people and seeing strange lands. I have come to the conclusion that while you are on a trip you don't know much about it—because you are so busy living it. It is only in retrospect that the trip's events come to you clearly and in perspective. For example, the long flight from Sydney, Australia, to London. It is even longer than it appears on the timetable, when you are "flying with the sun." A timetable may say that it is ten hours from one place to another. Yet you might have to turn your watch back two hours, so that actually you fly for twelve.

Although you think you are not noticing them, the noise and vibration of the plane can make you very tired. Also you eat a great deal. Hostesses are always feeding you. I also recall that during the flight from Sydney to Darwin I sat cross-legged in the dimly lit cabin of my plane and vaguely wondered what I was doing there. The seat next to mine was empty, and since the arm between the seats had been removed, I decided to stretch out and take a short nap. I had temporarily lost my shoes, having kicked them off, so that they now reposed under the seat of the very charming Dutch doctor who sat in front of me. I hadn't been getting enough sleep, and as I lay there I thought, "Let's face it, my girl, you are simply too old for this sort of thing."

In my stocking feet I staggered back to the lounge to wash my face. I thought I'd feel better if I freshened up. I found I was being followed by our hostess—an incredible girl who always looked cool, serene, and lovely. She asked if I felt all right and if I would like a cup of tea. Then she brought it to me and I drank it gratefully. How incredible this must sound—that one of the memorable events of my trip was a cup of tea at four-thirty in the morning. Yet I know why. It was a cup of tea sweetened and fortified by a warm personal kindness that went far beyond the requirements of merely efficient service.

"Tell us," insist my friends—who think me slightly mad because I did not go around taking snapshots—"tell us about the Hotel Raffles in Singapore. Tell us about breakfast in Cairo and lunch in Rome. Tell us about Bangkok." At this point none of these places holds much interest for me. My feeling is merely one of wonder that I was there at all. Throughout the flight I had a sense of almost complete unreality. "There's Bali," someone would say, pointing out the window. "There's Capri. The lake in that volcano crater is the highest in the world, over twelve thousand feet."

Now, if my friends had only asked me about churches . . .

Let me tell you about some of the churches I saw, such as the one on the island of Maui in the Hawaiian Islands. I flew from Honolulu to Maui, which I had never visited, to spend five breathless days with some old friends. One rainy day we set off on a sixty-five-mile drive through the mountains—along narrow, winding, precipitous roads, past rushing waterfalls.

On the way we stopped at a small Hawaiian church. The friend who drove us was acquainted with the church and its pastor—a Hawaiian woman who, although away at the time, had arranged for the church to remain open and for some of her congregation to be there. The church was set back from the road and high above the ocean. Never have I seen such colors: the sea an unbelievable blue, the bright white of the church, the green well-trimmed grass, and the little flower garden and shrubs that were cared for with such love and pride by the congregation. Three middle-aged women, in white dresses, came to greet us. They had sweet, brown, smiling faces, and they presented us with flower *leis*. We inspected their tiny cemetery above the sea, and then we entered the church. Waiting for us was a woman who was almost bent double with age. The other women, in their soft, liquid language, called her "grandmother." She was one hundred and two years old, yet her face had the extraordinary beauty often found in elderly Polynesian women. She had remarkably bright eyes, an alert mind, and she carried herself with great dignity.

We sat in the front pews of the church and silently prayed. The sound of the sea was far away, but the smell of flowers and salt air and sunshine permeated the church. One of the women then conducted a personal service for us. She prayed aloud in English and then in Hawaiian. Then we said the Lord's Prayer together and we sang an old hymn. Our acting pastor read from the New Testament in English, and finally she gave us a loving benediction. I have never attended such a service. And I don't think I ever shall again—unless I go back to that tiny village and again enter that little white church high above the beautiful sea.

After the service we went into the spotlessly clean church house for what we thought would be only coffee. It turned out to be a prearranged *luau*, or small feast. At each place was some baked taro. There was also pork cooked in *ti* leaves, dishes of seaweed and salmon, and finally coffee and cakes. As I ate I thought of the lunch basket we had packed with all the ingredients of a sumptuous American picnic. We had planned to have our picnic at a place where the road dips down to the sea and where the great black rocks are wildly lashed by the foaming water. We did go there an hour later, but we never touched a morsel of our picnic lunch.

After the *luau*, we thanked our hosts and went on to another church which my friends wished me to see. It was an old Roman Catholic church in a tiny community. Its interior walls had been painted an almost blinding blue. As we stood there we heard an ancient car come wheezing up to the front of the church. We went out to find the priest, a tall husky Belgian who had brought his dog with him. He explained that he had held a service earlier and had then gone off to hold another service in another community.

Many weeks later I stood in still another church that was just as unfamiliar to me—Westminster Abbey. It is beautiful beyond words, and so big that the two little Hawaiian churches would be all but lost in its spacious reaches. It was an overcast morning, and there were only a few people in the Abbey. As my companion and I went from one chapel to another, we had the feeling that the walls of this great church had been saturated with the spirit of worship, and that history was slowly seeping into our bones. We also visited one small chapel seldom visited by tourists—a rather bare, yet beautiful, room, named St. Faith's.

Later we went to visit St. Paul's Church, which

seems to stand guard over Fleet Street. We found a Christmas service for the children in progress. An enormous Christmas tree stood outside the church at the top of the steps. The sanctuary, itself, was crowded with children of all ages, accompanied by their parents. The youngsters joined with the choir in singing carols. Above their young heads, space soared to the great dome through which a bomb had exploded during the ugly days of World War II. A young boy, in a sweet child's voice, read part of the service. When he finished the children rose again to sing another carol.

As we were going down to the crypts, I noticed a man sitting alone in the very last pew. I couldn't tell if he was young or old. I could see only that he was battered and shabby, and that he had come to the end of a frayed and slender rope. I couldn't stop thinking about him. London in December produces a knifelike chill that cuts to the very marrow of your bones. Had this man wandered into the church to find a little warmth? Had some recollection of his childhood—happy or unhappy—brought him there? Would St. Paul's give him something more than merely physical comfort? I shall, of course, never know any of the answers. Yet I hope that this man took something away with him, possibly something he might have been seeking for years—for no one should be emptyhearted on the birthday of our Lord.

Moving through the crypts—and thinking of Lord

Nelson, the Duke of Wellington, and the young RAF flyer whose heroism is commemorated on a small bronze plaque placed in the wall near an imposing bust of George Washington—we finally came to a chapel which has also been dedicated to St. Faith. It is a much larger chapel than the one in Westminster Abbey, and I was told that it was frequently used for services during the war.

There was another place of worship I remember. On a day sharply whipped with rain and wind I went into the chapel of King's College at Cambridge University. No lights had been turned on, and in the darkness the magnificent stained-glass windows appeared like illuminated jewels with their brilliant, flashing reds and purple. Off this room was a smaller chapel, dedicated to the men who had died in World War I. I stayed for a long time . . . thinking of these men.

There are certain things—perhaps the word is imponderables—that are, so to speak, all of a piece in their continuity. Love, for example: love of God, of friend and stranger, of family, of country, of work and beauty. Worship is another continuity, a vast network, an endless reaching. It is also like a delicate, yet unbreakable, thread that stretches completely around the world. Everywhere I went I could feel this continuity of worship—from the little Hawaiian churches to the great Westminster Abbey to the chapel at Cambridge. Throughout the world you will find this thread. Wherever you find it you will also find vitality. The feeling of having once come close to it will never leave you. And when you return to your own familiar place of worship you will find it again. This is the reaching outward and upward that has been instinctive in man's heart and spirit since the beginning of time, man's spiritual hunger.

Jesus said, "In my Father's house are many mansions." Yet here on earth there are also many mansions, of all sizes, shapes, and qualities—and all built to His glory. I know my recollections of these places of worship will remain with me long after other memories of my journey have dimmed.

What you bring home from a journey is not the excitement, the strangeness of new situations, the adventure of distant places. It is, instead, the familiar to which you cling—the warmth and kindness of gentle friends, the courage and intelligence of everyday people, the unexpected generosity and thoughtfulness of strangers. And above all there is the awareness that when you pray and give thanks you do not do it alone.

JANUARY

1. ❀ *Midnight Conversations*

It has been some time since I have gone to bed and slept long and well. Usually I have wakeful nights only when I am overtired, or suffering some physical pain, or have just undergone a surgical operation. This past year, however, I have found myself repeatedly stalking sleep—and catching it only in snatches. I have tried the usual remedies, but with scant success. I don't find it relaxing, at three or four in the morning, to drink a glass of hot milk. And since I dislike sheep, I certainly don't enjoy counting them.

Sleepless nights, however, can have their value, if

you will just relax and lie quiet in the dark. Or you can turn on the light and read something you enjoy. On such occasions I invariably reach for my small Bible—and then the hours pass serenely, with the house big and silent, the darkness all about, and the quiet broken only by the whispering wind and the chatter of the birds as they wake with the rising dawn.

A sleepless night is a good time for thinking. It may be rather scattered thinking, for the mind is hard to discipline—but if you can sustain a related train of thought, it is astonishing how rewarding it can be. Just recalling happy memories can keep you occupied for a long time. Or you can, as I try to do, think a problem through to a helpful conclusion. Often I hit upon a series of brilliant ideas—which promptly dissolve into nothing with the coming of the dawn. But just as often I find ideas which withstand the searching glare of sunlight and are useful to me particularly as a writer.

On other occasions, just as I am awakening or falling asleep—in that twilight of semiconsciousness—I often experience a sense of being far beyond and out of myself, as if I were on the brink of solving every mystery and of knowing all there is to know with crystal clarity. But then I either fall asleep or come wide awake—and the moment, once again, is lost. This experience, I dare say, has happened to everyone. I believe it is a sudden realization of the eternal within us; something apart from the flesh, beyond the fallible mind, past the intellect, past even the heart with its profound and intuitive emotions.

Recently on a wakeful night I got to thinking about, of all things, vanity. I must admit that I've always been vain; most women are. In my case, however, I don't think I've ever been vain about my achievements, and certainly not about the workings of my mind. I don't fancy my mind overmuch. Nor have I been vain about any talent I may possess, for talent is something you are born with—a sort of bestowed gift. I have, however, been proud—which is not exactly vanity—of my ability to harness a small talent to a lot of hard work. Many a big talent has been lost or squandered because its owner has been either unable or unwilling to dedicate himself to his talent. Or because he has permitted himself to become frivolously concerned with less important matters.

My vanity is solely physical—possibly a personal fastidiousness, blown up to exaggerated proportions. I had a mother who was extremely dainty, besides being pretty and somewhat vain. And my father was the epitome of personal meticulousness.

Unlike most females, I am not particularly interested in clothes. I like them, but I hate to buy them —because I can't stand still long enough to be fitted. I also know what I want, and if I don't find it in twenty minutes I give up looking. I am rarely—which is remarkable for me—indecisive. No, with me vanity is not a matter of shop windows. As a girl it sprang from my desire to be thought attractive. And as a wife it derived from the wish to continue to be thought so. In later years I hoped my children would remember me as a well-brushed, well-dressed person. Then, too, there was the matter of having to make public appearances. I have always been vain—more or less secretly—of my small hands, feet, and bones in general and of the fact that I would never be fat, although there have been periods when a little less poundage would have been in order.

Lying in bed that night—with a cool wind coming through the open windows, the flowers in my room scenting the air, and a patch of silvery moonlight on the floor—I began to think of that quality, common to every human being, which we call soul or spirit. All my life I have known what I looked like—physically. For better or worse I know what my appearance has been and what it has become. But I haven't the least idea of what my soul looks like. You might say this is a ridiculous thing to think about. You might say that soul is soul and body is body, and that of course no one knows what his spirit looks like. I believe that when the day comes that I get a good look at my spirit I'm not going to like it very much. I wish I had thought of this sooner.

There are no cosmetics for the spirit. There is nothing you can buy to make it beautiful or even moderately attractive. You can't find anything on drug counters to enhance its appearance or step up its health and vitality. Whatever your soul may appear to be—to your Creator now, and eventually to yourself—it will be what you have made it, shaping and molding it with every thought, every word, every act of commission or omission. This is a frightening conclusion to reach on a sleepless night, or on the following day if the thought stays with you.

There's just no way you can hide the spirit, no way to disguise it. God, who gave it you, and who watches to see what you have done with the gift, has always known this. You can't clothe it in concealment. You can't blot out its blemishes. I believe that each dishonesty of thinking and acting—every unkind word, every fear, resentment, anger, injustice—plays a part in misshaping the spirit so that even the loveliest body can possess a twisted soul. Surely envy must bring spiritual wrinkles. Denial of good, acceptance of evil, lethargy which stills the tongue when it should be speaking in defense of right, laziness which robs us of responsibility toward a troubled neighbor, a troubled community, a troubled world—all these must mar and disfigure the soul. A sense of responsibility, like imagination, love, or even humor, is a spiritual muscle. If you don't exercise it, it becomes flabby, ugly, and eventually it atrophies.

How often have I heard people speak with bitter prejudice against those of another color, race, or creed—and have either kept cravenly silent or have merely tried to pour oil on the troubled waters. Why have I, again and again, committed this sin of omission? I, too, have had prejudices. But I've tried never to show them. And most of them I've succeeded in overcoming. But over and above this I have always known that, however I might feel about a prejudice, it has always been my responsibility to argue against it. Yet—and here again is vanity—because I've always wanted to be liked, because of my fear and hatred of unpleasantness and argument, I have kept silent. This—and it counts heavily against me—certainly cannot have enhanced my spirit, which, while invisible to me, is wholly visible to God. For as a man thinketh—and as he speaketh—so is he. Certainly, as you sow, so shall you reap.

Thoughts and deeds often break through from the spiritual to the physical self. All of us know people whose physical appearance, however attractive otherwise, is marred by discontent, ill temper, and selfishness. If these faults are so apparent on the surface, what must they be like deep in the souls of these people? Many of us have suddenly looked in a mirror and have been horrified to see upon our faces expressions which ill became us. But most of us have learned how to conceal our internal havoc with an agreeable manner and a false front of radiance. So, actually, there are no mirrors which can be held up to the spirit.

I have said hundreds of times, "I've just washed my hair and I can't do a thing with it." But who ever says that he has just soaked his spirit in egotism, petulance, and dishonesty, and now he can't do a thing with it?

You know how it is when you have your photograph taken. You want it to look the way you *hope* you look. I've had many a shock from seeing a candid picture of myself. I knew it was a photograph of me, but I could hardly believe it—and I certainly didn't want to. Perhaps this is how I will feel when my spirit is revealed to me.

There is, however, one thing which remains—and for which I pray. If the physical self has been neglected for many years, there is no chance of concealing this neglect no matter how many beauty counters you shop at or how many exercises you take or diets you follow. They may help a little, but only a little—for the main damage has been done. I fervently pray it will be otherwise with the spirit. It isn't easy to keep a guard over an unruly tongue, or to withhold hasty criticism, or to rise in defense of a moral or spiritual principle, or to take up cudgels for a friend or a stranger—especially when you haven't done these things in years, or perhaps have never done them. It isn't easy to switch suddenly from negative to positive thinking and to begin consciously to shape your thoughts for truth and beauty. Yet persistent attempts at self-discipline will eventually show in the spirit, however often these attempts may fail. If I am right, then when we take that first long look at what we, and we alone, have made of ourselves—for sorrows, circumstances, and disappointments are not really valid excuses—then perhaps we will not be quite so shocked as we first feared. Reshaping ourselves may result in a lopsided sort of creation, and certainly it will be far from anything approaching perfection. But at least we shall have tried—and that will be counted for us. For the Eternal Father is just. He knows our triumphs as well as our failures. He knows when we make the effort, even though we may not succeed. And always He is understanding.

And so should we be understanding in our human relationships. Someone once told me that "Judge not, that ye be not judged" suggested a dubious motive—a desire to be rewarded for being good—and that the line would be better translated if it read "Judge not, for ye also are on trial." It is an idea I shall not soon forget. To be understanding is to be forgiving. One of the most rewarding sentences of the Lord's Prayer tells us that as we forgive others, so shall we be forgiven.

A word I dislike is "tolerance." It carries an overtone of complacency and superiority. Instead of boasting, as we so often do, of being a "very tolerant person," I think it would be better if we merely tried to be understanding. Also, tolerance can be carried to a dangerous degree—to a degree where we lose sight of right and wrong. I believe there is a good warning against it in the words "Hate the sin, but love the sinner."

I suppose love is the real answer. If we can love people, even those we don't know, if we can love and care for the spirit within us which is God, if we can love upreaching ideas wholeheartedly, and if, most importantly, we can find within ourselves the pure love of God, then we can, however awkwardly, succeed finally in reshaping our spirit in His image.

2. ꕥ *My Favorite Character*

When someone asked me about my favorite among the fictional characters I have created I was delighted. For it gave me the chance to bring David Condit back from oblivion.

I do not especially like the word "created," despite its accepted use in connection with processes of thought, and especially with the arts. I believe that only God creates. Yet it is true that through Him and whatever gift He may have given us, we, being in His image, are permitted a sort of facsimile or carbon copy of creation. This applies not only to the arts, of course, but to the work of the scientist, the gardener who nurses the seed and grafts the branch in order to evolve a lovelier bloom or a finer fruit, to the carpenter who builds a good house, to every craftsman—and to everyone who puts his heart into the work he does.

Out of the sixty books I have written there is only one which, while it did not satisfy, at least pleased me, and the hero in that book is the most interesting of all my heroes to me. The book is called *American Family*, published by Farrar & Rinehart in 1935 after a serial version had appeared in *Cosmopolitan* magazine. The book is long out of print, obtainable only in libraries. It hasn't gone into a pocket edition.

Part of *American Family* is a fictionized family history—my own. I selected the name "Condit" because that, too, is a family name. I chose a background mainly of China and northern New York State: China because my grandfather and grandmother were missionaries there; northern New York because I had spent my summers there and knew the country.

My grandfather was born in 1838, and died in 1902. He went to China with his first wife, a child was born to them, but the young mother became ill. Grandfather brought her and the baby home, but the little wife died on the voyage and the baby girl was given to relatives to bring up. She was my half aunt, Josephine Baldwin, whom I dearly loved and who was for many years a well-known worker in the Methodist Book Concern.

Grandfather remarried and sailed for China in the American clipper *Hotspur* in June, 1862. During the long voyage my grandmother had a miscarriage, and so lost her first child. My father, her second, was born in the mission compound at Foochow. Several other children were born there, three of whom survived, and Father returned to the States briefly, as a toddler and again at eleven, traveling around the world with another lad and a tutor. After that he remained in the States, was educated here, and became a lawyer. When Grandfather returned from China, he became secretary of the Foreign Missionary Society.

Now, my father sometimes told me stories of his childhood in China, as did Grandfather and Grandmother. In their house in Brooklyn I saw many treasures they had collected, including the miniature sedan chair in which my father, and subsequent children, were carried. My father spoke Chinese before he spoke English; he indulged in various wild escapades, such as running away one day and spending much of the night in tiger-infested hills; he had close Chinese friends of his own age.

I had these memories secondhand, his letters written to his parents while he was on the grand tour, some diaries of Grandfather's, and a few letters from Grandmother to her mother, and from her mother to her.

Now, the journals kept by my grandfather during his tenure in China belonged to the mission and we did not have them, but some extracts were printed in old books and I was fortunate enough to run across these. In deciding that my hero's mother would also miscarry on the clipper voyage, I wondered *why*, and intensive reading disclosed the fact of the terrible storms through which the clippers rode to their ports. I had to know exactly what sort of voyage David's parents would have, and I decided to send them to China on Grandfather's ship, the *Hotspur*. I went to the public library and found a New York *Herald* dated June 16, 1864, and so learned at just what time the ship sailed on what sort of day, and who was the lookout at Sandy Hook.

As for the story, I used in Tobias Condit a man very like my grandfather as I had known him. His wife, Elizabeth, was, however, a figment of my imagination.

For the first part of the book—the voyage, the birth of the hero, David, in China, and like experiences there—I drew freely upon my father's diaries and the stories that had been told me. Like my father, my hero returned to the States. But then their stories became quite different, for, whereas my father became a lawyer, David became a doctor. My father wished never to return to China, but David's one burning desire was to go back.

I had to educate David, of course. So I educated him in New York and then at Wesleyan in Connecticut. Through a friend I met the historian of old Wesleyan and procured from him the book that treats of the college's first century. From the book and from talks with the helpful historian, I was able to picture accurately David's life at Wesleyan. From there I sent him to Yale as a medical student, which involved much correspondence with people at Yale and with a retired physician who had been, so to speak, in David's class. After Yale, David became an intern at Bellevue and this, again, meant reading, interviewing, and getting in touch with men who had interned there in the same years.

David's only wish was to return to China, to those whom he called his people, and to minister to them spiritually as well as physically. I saw to it, however, that he fell in love with and married quite the wrong girl, the ward of a well-to-do gentleman in New York, herself quite penniless, very pretty, remarkably shallow and spoiled, a product of her generation—or any generation.

David's interest in medicine had been increased by his friendship with a country doctor near Carthage, his mother's old home, where David spent his vacations. After he went to China to live and found his wife unhappy and dissatisfied, it was to northern New York State that he returned to take over the old man's practice.

David was always possessed by the dream that one day he would return to China, his work, and his friends. In the course of the story, his mother died and later his father, then he met again his wife's cousin, Anna, with whom she had been brought up. Anna had always loved David. But not until he returned to the States and saw her frequently, not until his wife's difficult and unhappy temperament had made him cognizant of his mistake, did he return Anna's love.

To a man of his nature, to a woman of Anna's nature, such a love was doomed from the beginning. Nothing could come of it, and nothing did. Later Anna married in England, and still later David's wife died.

In the book he married again, a woman much younger than himself. He had children by his first wife, Adeline, and by his second, Mary. His second wife he had known since her childhood, a farmer's daughter, a little girl who grew up adoring him and who through his help became a trained nurse. She brought him enormous happiness.

At the end of the book David and Mary are so situated that he can realize his dream. But the book ends in 1917, at the outbreak of the war, and David knows that he cannot return to China, that he must remain here, and be useful. The book ends in this way: "He told himself, these are my people. The dream, the stubborn dream, must die. There would be so little time for dreaming now. Perhaps there never had been."

American Family had the best reviews of any book I have ever written. The critics were kind, realizing that I had made a serious effort. But I recall that one of them found David "too good" and even said that he "would have liked him better had he gone out and gotten drunk a time or two."

This disturbed me briefly, but then I realized that it is harder, alas, to make a good man sympathetic, than it is to make a bad one despicable. Most people are agreed on what constitutes badness—or they were at that time. Perhaps they aren't now. But everyone seems to have a different idea of what is good in a human being.

Within my limitations, I made David as human as possible—with strong temptations and some impatience, with humor and laughter, and natural fluctuations of mood. He was devoted and kind to his wife, Adeline, but she sometimes tried him sorely. It would, however, have been quite out of character for him to have mistreated or to have left her; divorce would have been unthinkable. She had done nothing except be herself. She robbed him of his work and his dream because of her hatred for China. But she was his wife, she had borne his children, he had taken her for better or for worse, and he had a strong sense of responsibility. I do not believe that this *could* be overdrawn, one must take into consideration his background, his upbringing, his parentage and heredity, and above all, his deeply rooted religious nature. I see no reason why he should drink, any more than I see any reason why his love for Anna could come to any conclusion other than sacrifice and denunciation. It simply couldn't have been David.

David was the sort—in my conception of him—who is terribly needed in every community, large or small, and in any era. He was a good man, but he was neither smug nor self-proud. He tried, and sometimes he failed; but always he had in his spirit that refuge which is the dwelling place of God. What I endeavored to do was to draw a picture of an average man who believed in God, in family responsibility, in responsibility toward his work and friends. Despite the critics, and much earnest evidence to the contrary, I believe that such men are *not* unusual. I believe they are all around us, and that they exist in every walk of life.

FEBRUARY

1. ❀ *A.D.*

When I was young I used to make an elaborate set of New Year's resolutions. I don't any more, for —like most people—I find it easier to forget them than to keep them. Nowadays I aim at something more within my grasp, such as resolving to be a little kinder this year . . . a bit more patient, a bit more understanding. Or, like a child, I merely say, "I shall try to be good." For the main thing, I suppose, is trying. We fail every day, but if we keep on trying, surely it is counted for us.

Recently, when I was alone on Cape Cod in the loveliest little house I've ever seen, I had time to invite and examine my soul! What I saw I didn't like much, but at least I had time to think about it. I was fortunate in being about two minutes away from another writer, Gladys Taber, who is also one of my closest friends. We like the same things. We swam together and took her canoe out to paddle and fish. We enjoy the same food (Gladys is a fabulous cook) and we are both addicted to reading. Our literary tastes aren't always the same, but it is wonderful to sit and argue about them. And as writers we could "talk shop" by the hour and understand each other perfectly.

So the blue, green, gold days passed—sometimes with wind, often with fog, and twice the backlash of a hurricane. But always, to me, very wonderful. But occasionally what should have been a good day turned out to be a bad one, and I got to thinking about that, too. We all know such days when, for no reason the conscious mind can discern, we awaken depressed or restless or simply in our own personal fog.

I always wake very early on the Cape, usually with the first warm flush of sunrise on the water. I always get up and look across the green bushes, the inlet, and the sand bar to watch the pounding surf. Usually on such mornings—making coffee, going out on the sand terrace, feeding the birds—I feel a pure and mindless pleasure. I can look down to the house in which Gladys lives, and wave if she is out on the terrace. But then there are days, equally beautiful, when I stagger out to make coffee feeling as if I were caught in some kind of vise.

I dare say if we all kept charts we could see how the curve of our emotions rose and fell according to the weather, or what we'd eaten the night before. No one lives at the summit of his emotions every day in the week. And, indeed, not even for many hours in any one day. But then neither does one, if one is reasonably normal, live perpetually at the base of the mountain either.

I find that, while there are some people who are untouched by minor irritations but crack up under the big problems, the majority of us have quite the reverse make-up. We can face the big crises in our lives by somehow drawing on an inner strength but are completely thrown off balance by the trivialities. This is particularly true in our marital and parental relationships. The big things can be faced together, talked out together, drawing one upon the other for help and strength, and always turning to God in prayer or in the silent reaching out of the night. But the little annoyances—they are the everyday problems, the irritations, the frustrations, the exasperations—are mostly made by ourselves. Many a marriage and parental relationship has gone on the rocks (or come perilously close) simply because those involved weren't big enough to call out the spiritual reserves or weren't able to talk over their problems, even when they were trifling. As a rule, most people don't go to the inner temple of the spirit—that is, not until they have learned to ask for patience in small things as well as large. They can ask God to heal a deep wound or a dreadful illness—but not a scratch.

All of us—men and women, old and young—know such days. With children it's something that happens in school, a date gone wrong, a fancied slight, the refusal of something earnestly desired, whether it be a party frock or a Davy Crockett hat. It's the rain on the day the picnic's to be held; it's the new girl (or boy) in town whom you somehow can't impress. It's the tender confidence which is checked in mid-air by a busy mother or a preoccupied father. It's the disheartening discovery that even as a teenager you can be bored.

I don't know how it is with men; although I can think of some things that might upset them temporarily: coming home to an empty house, having a bad day at golf, or a worse one at the office, with the person they were counting on down with the flu, or a salesman coming in at the busiest moment.

With a woman it can be any one of a hundred things. The cream turns sour—or maybe you forgot to order it. The long-winded telephone conversation that keeps you from something really important. The expected letter that didn't come, or the one you hoped wouldn't come and did, the trivial wrangling with a tradesman, the children's pleading for something, the new dessert that looked so wonderful in the magazine picture and falls to nothing plus six when you get it on the table. (And wouldn't that be just the time for the man of the house to ask, "And why can't we have apple pie?") And then there are the days when you cut your finger, when your hair net literally goes out on a limb on your way to the clothesline in the back yard, when you can't get an appointment with the hairdresser, or when whatever you shopped for is delivered and turns out to be the wrong material or color, and you have to take it back. Nothing important, mind you—the bank hasn't failed, the mortgage hasn't been foreclosed, you haven't got a fatal illness, your husband hasn't left you. It's just one of those days.

Sometimes they seem very hard to bear.

I have had such a day. My hair net—gone in the high wind—was the last of a dozen I had brought with me. That was the day when, in my anxiety to find the last wild roses, I forgot to bring along gloves, completely ignored the thick tough brambles, and returned with much of me torn to ribbons. That was the day I awoke with a headache for no good reason, found the coffee tasting terrible, and couldn't look an egg in the face. That day I had to wait two hours to put through a call to my family, and particularly that day I dropped things—broke some of them—and most of them didn't belong to me!

On the Cape, Nature provides sun and salt air

and an indigo ocean. She creates spectacular dawns and superb sunsets and afterglows. The sea comes creaming in on the sand, and the little cove, white with gulls, is as quiet as a gentle heart. But on that day I could think only of scratches and telephone calls and broken cups and a blinding headache.

Had something serious happened I could have met it (as I met the snake—without fainting, although my fear is abnormal). I could have received bad news and quickly made plans—the bank, the taxi, the airport. But I couldn't seem to cope with the utterly unimportant, although knowing how unimportant it all was.

Headaches depart, scratches heal, hair nets can be bought at a dozen nearby shops, cups can be replaced, and if the telephone rings you can always just let it ring. The fact is that few really serious things happen in a lifetime. And also, we all have a reserve strength which operates subconsciously in emergencies. But little irritating things happen constantly. Hardly a day passes that at least one doesn't nip you like a gnat. And I suppose every so often, after you have shrugged them off for weeks, they finally pile up inside—and that's the day when everything goes wrong.

You often hear one woman say of another, "What a wonderful life she leads." And then she'll go on to tell of the other woman's wonderful husband, her wonderful children, her beautiful house, her exciting job. Maybe so. But how about those inevitable, nerve-jangling exasperations? I defy anyone to show me a person who is free of them. Everyone breaks things, gets a head cold, wakes with a headache, loses something, has friction in relationships—personal as well as impersonal.

I suppose the best thing for a woman to do is to get it out of her system by sitting down and having a good cry. Some people feel better by flaring up in anger, either at themselves or at the world in general.

At this time of year in my part of the world the ice lies along the branches and the snow comes feathering down. It's all very beautiful, and there are days when I seem to sparkle like a bright sun in a clear blue sky. But then there are days when I slip on the ice, get bogged hub-deep in the snow, or come down with the flu. It was Gladys Taber who said to me—one day we spent together and which had gone beautifully except for one small thing—"Well, nothing is perfect." I replied that if it were we would be all too reluctant to leave this world for one which has to be better—and how can you have better than perfection?

Because human beings are fallible, no human relationship can be perfect—nor can any life or any job—in fact, not even the weather. A beautiful scene can be flawed by the people you see it with or by a mosquito sailing into a gorgeous moonlight setting.

I question if anyone—however he may be endowed physically, mentally, or materially—ever achieves perfection in his lifetime. And I suppose that's as it should be. We grow and progress only by conquering our imperfections, those within us as well as those which result from the impact of external events. A perfect world filled with perfect people—much as we think we would love it—would probably be a crushing bore.

I don't want people to love me "despite" my faults nor "because" of them. I want my friends to take my faults in their stride, as part of my whole personality, and in so far as it is possible for them to do so, to understand the whys and wherefores of my faults. If each day brought only smooth sailing—with only an occasional choppiness in the water—we would learn very little, for the small lessons can teach us just as much as the big ones.

The remedy for the gnat bite or the scratch is to put something on it to relieve it. When the bite or scratch is on your mind, your heart, or your spirit, then I suppose the best remedy is hearty laughter—at yourself. If, at the end of what you believe has been a terrible day, you sit down and add it all up with pencil and paper—from the lost hair net to the broken cup, from the sheets which the laundry ripped to the belligerence of the tradesman (and how do you know he hasn't had a bad day too?), from the number of times your phone rang and it was always a wrong number—you will probably find that it hasn't been too bad a day after all. For against the list of your trivial irritations you will probably have some rather surprising items on the asset side —the unexpected mindfulness of a stranger, the flattering greeting from an old friend, the happy circumstance which solved a bothersome problem. You may well find dozens of things that were good as against the few that weren't. Things usually balance. At times the scales may tip far up or far down. But in the long run they balance.

February is the month in which New Year's resolutions are usually abandoned. I think it is the month in which they should be reaffirmed. My New Year's wish for you is the same one I'm wishing for myself. We know there will be "good" days and "bad" days. I hope we can meet the serious things with strength and fortitude and the trivial ones with the inner laughter that will put them in their proper place. The important thing is to go forward, not to regress or even just mark time. No one knows what the next year, the next day, the next minute will bring. No matter what it is, we can learn from it—if we keep ourselves geared to learning. We may not know we have learned the very instant it happens, nor that day, nor possibly that year. But someday we will.

I truly wish you a happy New Year—and that at the end of it, when you "balance up" the preceding twelve months, you'll discover what you have gained and what you have lost, what you have learned and what you have yet to learn, what you have met with courage and what you have met merely with irritation. Happiness is not for every minute of every hour. It is a flash, a wonder, a reaching up. It is no more stable than we are, and not to be captured and held any more than a wild bird that darts past us on its way to the far horizon. Happiness is a sudden gift out of the blue. Contentment, however, is something else again. It is stronger stuff, less exciting but a great deal more enduring.

And so I wish you happiness—contentment's elusive sister—and I also wish you contentment itself, that it may walk beside you enduringly. For it does, you know, only half the time we don't stop to think about it. Contentment is taking things as they come: love, work, the beauty all about us and the knowledge that, although heaven may seem far away, He who created it, as well as the earth and ourselves, is as close to us as the air we breathe—as ready, as simple, and as accessible to all of us as that.

2. ✤ *Communication*

It is fascinating to contemplate communication and the different forms it assumes. The tremendous importance to us all of the many types of communication did not occur to me before. Or, if it did, I took it for granted, as we do so many things.

For example, when I write this journal I am communicating with you who read. I am thinking about you as I write. I am wondering if I say the right things and if something will move you to agreement, argument, approval, or disapproval.

Writing in any form is a means of communication—sometimes good and sometimes, unfortunately, not good. Writing is a form of what we term art. But I dare say the one universal form of art is music. Here is something which goes out and finds almost everybody. There are many people who do not care for reading, but only a few who really dislike music. Of course, we do not all like the same kind of music. I, for one, do not enjoy very modern music and the so-called "hot" type. I do not understand this kind of music, and it is harsh and irritating to my ears. But many of my friends like it perfectly. To them it is not only a pleasing sound but a good one.

At any rate, though all of us have preferences in music, the majority, of whatever race or nationality, enjoy deeply some or many forms. Thus strangers who do not speak each other's language can sit, side by side, in a concert hall or at a radio and be in communication with each other because of the comprehended bond of the music

Painting is something else again—and once more we are not agreed upon what constitutes greatness. I suppose that the whole matter, whether we speak of writing, music, or painting, comes down to the essential element: the reader, the listener, the person who sees. Without these there would be no art of any kind. There must be someone to send. But also there must be someone to receive. So, whatever *moves* the man whose eyes follow the print or rest upon the canvas or whose ears hear the sounds of the instrument *is* great, whether by critical standards or not. If I read a book, hear a melody, look at colors on the canvas, and feel the small, authentic shiver in my blood that means I think I understand what the writer or musician or artist is trying to express—understand it in my own way, whether this is his way at all—then, whatever I read, hear, or see is authentic art as far as I am concerned. I may be the only one who thinks this, or greatly in the minority, but for me it is true. And that matters, very much.

Conversation is the most prolific means of communication, of course, and yet most of us have found that words can be used as blocks in the path of understanding. "Semantics" has been a subject for discussion for some time, most of us not greatly understanding what the word means. But anyone can understand how hard it is to be understood. We speak a simple sentence using common words with, we think, common meaning only to find that our listener has made quite another—and yet to him true—interpretation.

It is said that we do not make our friends, that we simply recognize them. I believe that we are drawn to those people with whom we can readily communicate, people for whom the words we use contain the exact, or nearly exact, meaning with which we employ them. I have often thought of the enormous importance of communication in human relationships.

In the parental relationship, for instance, there is often so little real communication, no matter how much parents and children are concerned for each other's well-being, that the value of the relationship is in danger. As for marriages, I am convinced that many go on the rocks mainly because of lack of communication.

This is not to say that a husband and wife do not talk! One may be more articulate than the other, and usually is—and not always the woman! Yet to be articulate is not necessarily to be able to communicate. Sometimes there is greater lack of communication in facile talking than in silence.

The one form of communication in all relationships that is paramount is selfless, warm, outgoing love. But sometimes only one member of the partnership is able to send, and not all people are able to receive.

Nor is all communication personal; some is impersonal, but also vital. Consider the communication between a nation and its government, between the peoples of different nations. I dare say that one cause of the endless, brutal wars is lack of communication.

I just looked at the package of unanswered letters upon my desk and thought of how easily written words may be misunderstood. The writer may be misunderstood. The writer may mean one thing and the reader misinterpret. Here, again, we come into the dangerous domain of the use of words as a means of conveying an idea, an opinion, or stating what to the writer seems to be a simple truth.

Sometimes it is a matter of mood, time, and circumstance. If you are in, say, India, doing important things, and I am at home doing what I believe are also important things, and I sit down to write you what I am doing, how I am feeling, what the world seems like to me at the moment, it will be some time before you get my letter, despite air mail. So, when you read it, perhaps your mood is as far removed from mine as the sun from the earth. I shiver in the country's cold winter; you are baking under an alien sky. It is the wrong time of day, or you have had a wretched night. It is impossible for you to share my enthusiasm for popcorn, sleigh rides, or toasted marshmallows. It seems trivial to you that yesterday I had tea with Mrs. So-and-so and tomorrow I am attending a Board meeting. Perhaps, had I reached you when you were in a different frame of mind, you would have been interested and sympathetic, but as it is you are a little bored. So, no matter what I have said or how many stamps I have used, I have not communicated with you, after all.

The one person who can communicate on paper with the certainty of a snake striking or a sledge hammer falling is the poison-pen writer. People who take their pens in hand anonymously are always craven. The sane, however hostile, people who sit down to write an unpleasant letter will sign their names and give the reader a chance to explain, justify, or simply fight back. But a writer who refuses to sign his name and hides behind an envelope, a stamp, and a blob of ink is more cowardly than any snake. The snake strikes impersonally, because it is threatened, disturbed, or frightened. Not so the anonymous letter writers. They strike in order to expel their bane and poison.

These letter writers are at one end of the scale. But the communication of unkindness takes many forms, most of them "signed" in some way or another—a casual spoken word, a look of indifference, criticism, boredom, a shrug, thoughtless gossip. All of us have been guilty of these things time and again. It's all communication, and on the wrong side.

We communicate in so many ways. A smile will do it or the opposite of a smile, a gesture, even the way we reveal our irritations in such a simple act as opening or shutting a door. There is no time in the day except when we are alone that we are not communicating, consciously or not, with someone else.

No, I'm wrong. Even when we're alone we're in communication—with ourselves, through the stream of consciousness. And what are we telling ourselves? Are we flattering or praising, being sorry for or excoriating ourselves with regret or shame?

Yet at the same time we are probably thinking of people and events which could make us happy.

It works both ways, communication.

There is one supreme form which is available to us all, and of which we do not take sufficient advantage. It is silent, as a rule. It is our personal communication with God.

Prayer does not have to be spoken. It can be thought—in the quiet room, on the busy street, at a typewriter, behind a counter—anywhere we go and no matter what we are doing. For it comes from the still place within us, the sanctuary each of us possesses, and it goes directly to the Listener who never tires. Who always understands. For thought is surely the swiftest communication.

Again, you are in India. I am here. I think of you and I am also in India. There is no distance that cannot be traversed by thought. It has been said that two people may be together, yet, because of the hostile shape of their thoughts, so apart that they inhabit distant stars; and two who do not even inhabit the same world may be so close in their thinking that they are side by side.

And when thought is prayer, you are where God is.

"Goodbye" is a word we use carelessly. It means "God be with you," as I think I have said before. It is a lovely word, yet superfluous. Because He is, always, closer than hands or feet. And thinking is the communication, the pathway.

For the thought that shapes the deed is more important than the deed itself. Perhaps we shall be judged one day upon our thinking, and upon the manner in which we have conveyed it. For everything is there—our kindnesses and cruelty, our wisdom and stupidity, our love and hostility, our prejudice and understanding.

As a man thinketh, so is he; and as he communicates his thoughts, by whatever means, in such measure does he affect himself and everyone he meets and knows, whether for better or for worse.

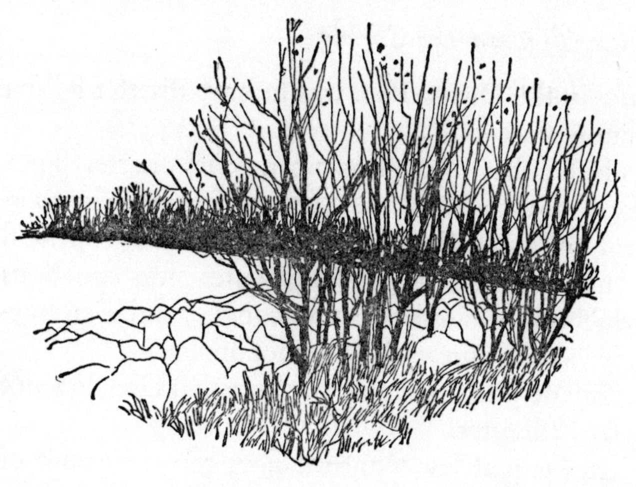

MARCH

1. ❀ *Bare Bough but New Leaf*

For some time I have been thinking about writing this. Frankly, I haven't wanted to because for the first time in my life I haven't known exactly what I wanted to say or precisely how to say it.

Some years ago a friend of mine told me, "I believe you attract disaster." Well, I don't believe that and I never have. I think that many of us attract a number of things: people, friends, success, happiness—but only if we work for them. Some, they say, attract luck. That's as may be. But I doubt if anyone really attracts disaster. And that includes Job, whose role in the Divine Plan was to have disaster fall on him repeatedly.

I do believe that people can court disaster. They can ignore traffic signals, they can leave a cellar stairway unlighted and unmended. Or, on a less physical plane, they can deliberately enter into situations which can end only in sorrow, regret, and even tragedy, both for themselves and for others.

But despite the cynics, I believe that God does not *will* us disaster.

In the past few months I have run the gamut of nearly every emotion, from despair, hope, happiness, and deliverance back to despair and the most appalling grief I have ever known—a grief which includes everything it shouldn't: resentment, unacceptance, rebellion.

That there has been a Plan in all this I *do* accept, and I have no quarrel with it whatever. Also I realize as the difficult days pass, all too slowly, that there has been a measure of compensation. Perhaps that isn't the right word, for I don't feel compensated. But I am grateful for my new discoveries in the outpouring of love that has come to me from those close to me. I have found a much closer closeness.

But what has been brought home to me most forcefully is my own weakness. There is no phrase in the Bible which I can more knowingly interpret than the one which reads, "Lord, I believe, help thou mine unbelief." Never until now have I fully understood that sentence.

For many years I have, as the saying goes, been "helping" people. It therefore astonishes me that I am now unable to help myself. I have written and spoken hundreds of thousands of words which have been described as "inspirational." I meant every one of those words—but, as far as inspiration is concerned, at the very moment I have none either to give or to receive.

I remember also that in my personal letters and published works I have sincerely urged people to accept and adjust, and to pray for peace and understanding of those blows from which they feel they will never recover. I have reminded them that it has been promised that recovery will one day be theirs. Those to whom I have personally written and who have read my published writings have thanked me for all I said, and have assured me that it helped.

I hope it really did. For I must now add that in recently answering literally hundreds of extremely kind letters I have been unable to tell the writers that they have helped me—because, frankly, they have not. I am grateful beyond expression for their genuine concern. But there it stops.

So, now I am learning another difficult lesson. Help, if any, lies not in the love of one's family nor the concern of one's friends, but within one's self. The tragedy is that when I look within myself, expecting to find restoring factors—endurance, strength, courage, acceptance—they just aren't there. This is not to say I have lost my belief in God or in the promises of Jesus. I have not. Prayer comes as easily as ever—but it is prayer without words, demands, or petitions.

I have also learned to live a day at a time, and to ask only for endurance sufficient for that day. It is, I think, about all I can now expect.

Not long ago I wrote a book. Some of you may remember it. It was called *The Juniper Tree*, and was published in September 1952, after I had spent sixteen years dreaming about it and planning it. It concerned a man, lost in the starless night of sorrow because of the death of his only son, and his slow struggle back to something resembling an ordered mind and an acceptance of his loss. At the time I wrote the book I thought I knew all there was to know about sorrow, even though I had viewed it from a detached angle. I have always been able, sometimes unfortunately, to wear the other fellow's shoes, to walk in his path, and to experience in print what he has actually experienced.

Now I find I know nothing whatever about grief—except from the remote viewpoint of an amateur psychologist.

It is like having been blind. The man born blind puts his sensitive hands around, say, a tree. He feels the texture of the bark, he touches the leaf, he runs his fingers along the bough. He is aware of the cool wind, the warm sun, he hears the bird's song. A friend stands beside him and describes the tree. In this way he has, in the valiant language of the blind, *seen* it.

But, of course, he has not seen it. Let us say that one day his sight is restored, not the sight of a man who once had sight, lost it, recovered it, and who during his blindness always had memories of mental images. But a sight which never really was. I suspect that to his now sighted eye the same tree will be quite different.

Now at last I have seen the tree, not merely through the hands of my imagination and the words of people who know about trees—but with my own shocked, incredulous eyes. I assure you, it looks wholly different.

A while back I spoke of compensations. I have always believed, for example, that I was a leaner; that I couldn't, or wouldn't, stand on my own two feet and that, except in certain instances, I was unable to make decisions and assume responsibility. In recent months I have learned that none of this is true. Granted, I have never liked making decisions. As with most mildly neurotic people, trivial decisions have always come hard to me—what dress to wear, what coat, shall I take my rubbers, what train should I catch, and is it to be lamb chops or hamburger. Things like that. I remember in my early married life that I used to wander into my small son's room at night and wonder if he should have an extra blanket. I usually wound up consulting his father, a man of decisive action, who would say yes or no without hesitation. If he said no, I would go on my way feeling that if the child awoke with pneumonia the next morning at least it wouldn't be my fault.

This indecisiveness has carried over into my later life. I have always found it easy to place my problems in the hands of a businessman, a lawyer, a friend—anyone more capable than I.

Recently, however, I have been called upon to make many decisions, most of them vitally important. I have had helpful advice, but in the final analysis it was up to me to say yes or no. And I have found that it was not so hard, for I was deciding what seemed best for someone who was dependent on me for my decision.

Now at last I know that, much as I dislike it, I can make my own decisions whether they be trivial or grave. It doesn't matter if it is calling a doctor, having something done to the house, or completely altering my life. I can do it.

In the past few months my life has been drastically changed. I have lost my husband, and somehow my whole life has become infinitely complex. The reconstruction is not small.

Not long ago I found myself living happily in the city in what I considered were restricted quarters. I planned to live there for the better part of each week, and for all the winter months. This decision took me no time to make, and caused me no anguish—because the important thing was not where or how I lived but with whom I would be living.

Now I am back at the house, and whether or not I go to the city in the bitter winter months is entirely up to me. It's a bridge I'll cross when I come to it, confident that I can cross it alone.

As I write, the northwest wind is cool, the sun warm and dazzling. It is a beautiful day, but I am not yet ready for beauty. I cannot look upon it except with a wholly impersonal pleasure, with a sort of lip service. In fact, I look upon it very little. I am deprived, or have deprived myself, of a great many things dear to me, from moonlight to music, from books (for the first time in my life I cannot read) to motion pictures which, when they were good, I always enjoyed.

This, I suspect, is an angry sort of withdrawal from the world—which has to go on no matter how I feel about it. Yet I am reasonably certain that I shall gradually return. I have never believed that "time" is a healer, but I do believe it helps. Sometimes it can play tricks—and tragic ones—but it does help.

What I know I must look for on the bare bough is the leaf . . . it will not physically be there, yet somehow it must be enfolded within, incorporated, asleep, waiting, and in its essence, alive. When spring comes it will emerge, the pale-green wonder. But the real wonder will be that it has been there all along. This I know with my mind.

Therefore, at the start of the year I shall begin to look for spring, knowing that spring has always come, that there must always be resurrection. There is more hope for me in that than I can possibly express. The winter heart, bare as the bough, also must experience springtime and renewal.

Several things sustain me. I believe there must have been a Divine Reason for a Divine Plan, and that the Plan still operates. Another is the fact that some time ago someone I love, and still love, said to me for no reason whatever, "Such courage!" I have never known why those words were said. They came at a moment of peaceful happiness—and I forgot to ask. But they are enough to go on. The fact that they were quite erroneous is of no moment. Therefore I live by the Plan, and two words, and these will see me through.

2. ❀ *Other People's Problems*

One requirement of a successful fiction writer is that he must be able to get his characters out of all sorts of perplexing troubles. Professionally, this is an invaluable talent. But personally it is a dangerous one, for in developing a facile knack for solving his characters' problems the writer is often lulled into also believing that he can solve his own problems just as easily.

There is another danger to this talent. Impressed by his seeming omniscience, an author's readers will decide that he can also solve *their* problems with the mere flick of a finger. I, for example, have been asked to pay off more mortgages, buy more pig farms, put more children through school, set up more people in business, and pay for more hospitalization than anyone else I know—except, of course, a number of other writers. Fiction readers are generally convinced that writers never have the problems that harass "ordinary" people. This, I think, stems from two other false notions: One is that writers are constantly being snowed under by fat checks from publishers. And the other is that writing isn't work anyhow—and if you just know a lot of big words all you have to do is lay them down end to end until you finally come up with a best seller.

There are, of course, writers who make a lot of money. But very few make it right off the bat—with their first book or magazine serial—and then go on making it at a steady clip. Most writers have to work for years before arriving at the point where their output is in demand. And even then—as with most artists—it's a case of having a feast today and a famine tomorrow. A writer may spend seven lean years on a book—during which he also slaves at a regular job to keep himself and his family in food—and then suddenly find he's produced a best seller. This, however, is not the end of the rainbow. His highest financial returns on the book will come during the first two years—and because they *are* high, they will be laid low by income taxes. Revenue authorities—who seem to have the usual delusions about writers—simply cannot see why, because a book may have required seven years of work, its financial rewards should also be spread taxwise over seven years. I have often spoken against this injustice—and invariably met with the most bewildering reactions. Either my listeners are upset by my "notions" or—apparently in the belief that I am seeking special privileges—they become downright affronted. No matter how carefully I explain the facts to them, they insist on believing that any writer who is fairly well known must necessarily have gathered unto himself—and is now hoarding—all the gold in Fort Knox.

Readers' problems, however, are not always financial. Often an author is asked only for advice. And here is where a writer is liable to fall into a second trap. Since everyone enjoys the lofty role of being a wise and seasoned counselor, it is difficult to remember that few people who ask for advice really want it. All they actually want is to be told that a certain course of action—to which they've already made up their minds—is the right one.

There was a time when—rushing in where angels fear to tread—I responded to readers' problems with the greatest desire to be helpful. Now I'm on the side of the angels, for you can get into a lot of trouble giving advice to strangers. Many years ago I ran an "advice" column under an assumed name in a small magazine. I recall a letter from one woman who wrote that her husband regularly beat her and her children, and then threw her downstairs just to complete his morning exercise. She wanted to know what I thought she should do. The gist of my advice was to take herself and her children and depart forthwith. Apparently no advice could have been more naïve. My hard-bitten editor, who read my letter, scathingly pointed out that, while my advice might well save the woman's life, it would also give her husband excellent grounds for suing the magazine for alienation of affection. Shortly after that I was fired.

Trying to be a helpful adviser has still another serious danger. Seldom are you permitted to see the "other side of the story." In the instance of the much-pummeled wife—which seemed an open-and-shut case if ever I'd heard of one—I didn't stop to consider that possibly, when the husband was in a soft and peaceful mood, his wife attacked him like a tigress and succeeded in throwing him down the front stairs.

Whatever the situation, the fact remains that it is often possible to be of real help to another, for the truly great problems of life are basic—those of sorrow, faith, love, fear. This isn't to say that you can solve another's problems. You can't. No one really solves anything except for himself. But usually you can help, for most of us have had these experiences ourselves. And you can genuinely say to a troubled friend, "I understand. I have been through the same trouble—and this is the path I took. It may help you to find your own way."

People often write me that they are not "understood," and are lonely and unloved. It's not hard to see why. If you can't give love, you can't expect to receive it. And, actually, no one understands anyone completely—including himself. Self-understanding, in fact, is the hardest problem of understanding. Yet people are always demanding that other people understand their innermost feelings in their most delicate shadings.

I have an old and dear friend whom I consider an exceedingly wise man. Many people bring their problems to him—but often they are problems which I feel are extremely trivial. When I asked him how he could afford to waste his time and patience, he replied, "The problems may seem insignificant to you, but they're not trivial to the people who are confronted by them. Often these people are without the security they need—at home, with their friends, in themselves, or in a deep religious faith. Yet it is astonishing how merely by listening, by being concerned, by saying a word here and there, it is possible to 'put them back on their feet' so that once again they can stand by themselves with assurance and confidence."

Since people often go to total strangers with trifling problems, it is entirely likely that they bring the same kind of problems to God in prayer. A child, for example, will pray, "Please don't let it rain on the day of the picnic." We are tolerant of the child because we know that he has no awareness of the immutable laws of nature. Also, the child has rightly been given an abiding faith in God—to whom nothing is impossible. But things can also be impractical. The rain that drowns out the child's picnic can be the greatest blessing to the farmer who has looked at the sky day after day and prayed for the life-giving rain that will save his dying crops.

Many people carry their childhood far into adult life. Often they have told me of things for which they have prayed—a new frock, a pearl necklace, a vacation they can't afford, the resignation of a disliked boss. Almost always they pray for things which they make no effort to earn. Why they should expect these things to be handed to them on a silver platter, I'll never understand. I've always believed that God helps those who help themselves. What I say is—earn the dress, settle for something less than pearls, take a vacation you can afford, and either learn to get along with your boss or find a new job. If you put your shoulder to the wheel and shove hard, your prayer will have just that much strength to it. I used to pray for all kinds of things for my children. Now I ask of God only that He show them how to help themselves, how to solve their own problems, how to earn their own happiness.

Now comes spring with its cold rains, its warm sun, and the wind blowing and beating . . . with promises kept one day and broken the next. And suddenly the snow and frost are gone, and everywhere you look you find something green. Yet the grass, the flowers, the trees slipping leafy bracelets out along their arms—none of these grew by themselves. First there had to be a seed or root that was planted by man or nature. And then the plant had to grow. And in growing it had to struggle against threats and dangers—insects which prey upon tender leaves, blizzards which can freeze, summer suns which can scorch.

In all nature, nothing lives without a struggle. A plant survives by adaptation, and trees must bend with the wind. Man, however, has been given the gifts of intelligence and free will. And he must assume the responsibility inherent in these gifts. He knows, or should know, that much of life will be a painful struggle. To some problems he will—like the plants and trees—be able to adapt and bend. But not to all. And where he can't, he will have to put his will and intelligence to work.

Because it made me feel wise and important, it used to be a lot of fun having people ask me for my advice. But not any more. Now I find myself humbly telling these people, "Look within yourself for your solution. Go to your faith in God for guidance.

Search your own past for the answer to your present problem. And don't always stay within yourself. One of the best ways to be happy and to reduce your own problems is to extend your heart and mind into the problems of others, and help them work out their difficulties in the only way that is worth while to them—with their own solutions."

In the last analysis the burden of mankind's destiny is on the doorstep of mankind itself. God has given man the power of decision—and the responsibility of making decisions, for better or for worse, with respect to himself and his fellow man. And so, whatever else we may be, we are most certainly—for better or for worse—our own and our brothers' keepers.

APRIL

I. ✿ *Rebirth*

Now that April is here to remind us of the annual triumph over winter, I suppose, as we emerge into the longer light, winter is almost forgotten. But I cannot soon forget, looking at the scars of the January ice storm here in New England which ripped great branches from our enormous mulberry tree and from the maples. And the same storm sent an apple tree crashing to earth. That storm period is not easily forgotten, with the sharp sound of sleet on the panes, the trees and shrubs and power lines sagging and thick with ice, and then the dreadful noise of the branches snapping and falling in the night. Later the clamor was worse, for the ice loosened and fell and there was a cannonade all night as it hit against the frozen crust of snow. I lay awake in darkness—for in my section there was no electric power for over forty-eight hours—and listened to it with fright and awe.

But now April runs green along the awakening bough, the air is chilly sweet, and the birds begin to sing. So, wherever there is spring there is rebirth. Soon the scars will be blossomed over and we will scarcely know that the storm has come and gone.

It is April and Easter—the words which, spoken together, are so melodic and joyous.

But all year round, whatever the season, there can be rebirth. Spring is but a symbol, and Easter commemorates the victory over death as spring marks the emergence from destructive winter. Every day, perhaps every minute, somewhere in the tired world a spirit is reborn.

Perhaps it is merely a weary spirit, struggling toward and attaining a rebirth of endurance, or a timid one, achieving the renascence of courage. Many of us, myself among them, need and pray for this courage throughout the year. Sometimes it is a rebirth into faith which means God, and God is hope.

The sins, big and small, the flaws and faults that

weigh down and hamper the spirit, that clip its soaring wings, must perish before the soul is born anew. Sometimes there are just little things: the tongue given to quick unkindness, to petty gossip; the heart, which withholds words of simple endearment, praise or gratitude; the soul, sick with envy, yet longing for health.

I know of a woman who is ill and who is aware that she is causing her own pain and suffering. She is both envious and resentful and acknowledges it. Years ago, while engaged in professional work of another sort, she began to write. She has told me that her writing was of no real importance, and yet was accepted by the editors to whom she submitted it. But then a change came in her family situation, with illness and heavy expenses. It became necessary for her to earn a living, and because it promised more certainty and security, she returned once more to her original profession, giving up the weaving of her fiction fantasies. When she was away from home, she worked hard. When she was at home, she nursed, cooked, and kept house. And, at night, she fell into bed too tired to dream, even of the heroes and heroines, and tired, too, from frustration. For nothing makes you as bone-tired as that.

There was another woman, with whom my friend had gone to school, and who was, she says, the ultimate in charm. She was also, or so my friend thinks, the essence of insincerity. She began to write at the same time my friend did and has since become very successful. Not only materially successful, but she has achieved critical acclaim and prestige.

What poisons my friend's life and thinking is the fixed belief that—had it been permitted her—she could have done so much better, been more successful than her schoolgirl acquaintance. The knowledge of this other woman's success actually makes her ill. She cannot bear to read of it, nor see the name mentioned. She is intelligent, and so she wonders if this gnawing resentment has not caused the physical pain that is always with her.

Very likely it has. I do not know much about psychosomatic medicine, but I am convinced that envy and resentment, jealousy and hate can be lethal. They are slow killers. They cripple. They are parasites which murder their host.

But I wonder. Has my friend stopped to think of that other envied woman as a person and not merely as a symbol of the success she herself has craved and missed? For my friend has a family, every member of which loves her. And she has a profession which has brought her affection and respect. On all counts, despite her struggle, hers should be a happy spirit.

I do not know, but perhaps the writer she so envies is not a happy woman. For who knows what she lacks or wishes, or what is poisoning *her?* Who knows another's soul? Who truly knows the spirit, the despair, the desperation and anxiety of those nearest him?

And who, if he knew, would ever envy? For each of us has his burden, his failures, and his very special blessing. It is an old saying that the back is fitted to the burden and that the cross each of us bears is ours alone.

My friend has many blessings, and these, if she will see them with her humble heart, will bring about her cure. Perhaps her great physical disease will not be healed, but her spiritual illness will lessen, perhaps even vanish. And her crippled spirit—so much more tragic than the crippled body—will find its wings once again.

This woman of whom I write I have never met, but she has written me and given me permission to tell you all this. She says, "It may help someone else." Nor do I know the name of the person who is unknowingly her deadly enemy. Even so, I think I understand.

Often in my life I have wished that another's success was my own. I don't believe I have envied it. But I do have moments of wishful thinking. I have never wanted anything belonging to anyone else, but simply, and childishly, something *like* it. Sometimes it has seemed to me (when the going has been extra hard) that success came too easily to others; yet I know this was not true. Success does breed success, so to speak, but the original effort and struggle have seldom been easy for anyone.

Then, too, during the times when I myself have

been successful enough materially to satisfy anyone, I have wanted the other side of the moon, the prestige and the critical applause. But not many people have both sides—the side the bread is buttered on and the side that is spread with a special manna!

Yes, I understand this woman. I wouldn't say to her, "Be content with your lot," because that's a vegetable sort of state and wouldn't really solve her problem. Her task, as I see it, is to face herself squarely and to evaluate all that she has against that which she has not—perhaps written down in two columns. She will find, as we often do, that the assets far outweigh the liabilities.

There is no healing for the wounded mind and the maimed spirit save in God, and to find Him, I believe, we have to struggle through self. For it is as a wall between us and Him. Once we have broken through, the way is much clearer. Perhaps a door has been shut against us, upon which we have hammered until our hands bled and have cried until our voices faltered and finally stopped. I know I have experienced this and I think many of you have also. But the trouble is, we are always fixing our strained attention upon that one door, we do not see any other. If only this particular door would open, we think, we would be in our own special Eden, our personal garden full of light and scent and sun. But all the time there are *other* doors which would, if we would only turn from the sealed one, swing open at the pressure of a finger and show us vistas undreamed of, far more lovely than any we have ever imagined.

When we repair our flaws, when we atone for the sins, when we are made aware that there are doors not meant for us to open, and seek other outlets—then the spirit is born again. And we experience, whatever the season, the surge of April in our hearts and minds and souls. We have become a part of the rebirth, which, in turn, is part of God Himself.

It is the risen Christ, the fulfillment of His promise. And so it is with the human soul reborn to hope and given new courage.

We think of the coming of a new year as another chance, the slate wiped clean, the beginning all over again, whether or not we make formal resolutions. But we think also of spring as an end and a beginning—an end to the dark short days, the storms and depressions of the winter season, and a beginning of beauty, warmth, and re-creation.

And so it is. For now, as I have said, the scars are hidden by new growth, the sap runs, the shrub considers putting forth its fragile bloom, the tree prepares to offer refuge to the singing bird and shade to the weary. The fruit blossom is still closed like a fist against us, but it will open and later there will be fruit.

All this, and more, the spring presages, promises, and fulfills. But there is no time of year, any year, when the spirit cannot be reborn to its own personal springtime, however dark the hours that have just passed.

2. ❀ *A Praying Woman*

There has come to my desk a letter from a *Christian Herald* reader. She signed her name but did not give me her address, so I could not thank her for it. I am thanking her for it now.

In the letter she said, among other things, that she wished I would pray for her; she ended, "I know you are a praying woman."

I have thought about this phrase ever since. It seemed to open doors for me, to cause me to ponder deeply the great subject of prayer. And now as we enter into the joyous hope and fulfilled promise of the Easter season, the eternal resurrection, I would like to share some of my thoughts with all of you.

I don't suppose, until now, I've thought of myself as a "praying woman." Most of us say our prayers, aloud or in our hearts, in church and at home, morning and night. We also say them when disaster threatens, when we are distraught by fear or sorrow, when there is something we need or overwhelmingly desire.

We say, often, that many of our prayers go unanswered. Some of us lose our belief in God. Long ago, a young woman said to me, "I don't attend church any more; I don't believe in God. During the war, I went into church every day and prayed for my husband's safety and that he would return to the children and me. He did not. Why should I believe in anything?"

It is difficult, perhaps impossible, for the vast majority of human beings to see the over-all picture clearly. And it does, indeed, take tremendous and unshakable faith to remind yourself that God does not make the wars which kill men.

Another friend, speaking of personal loss, said to me, "How often and deeply I prayed! They say nothing is impossible to God. Still He didn't raise His hand to help me."

Nothing *is* impossible. This I believe. I believe that God can halt the storm, save the plane hurtling downward in flames, bring the ship to port, heal all human misery. More. He can prevent it.

Then, they ask, why doesn't He?

I am just an average woman. I don't know. But I can guess. In the first place, we were created human, with free wills, with the power to decide things for ourselves. Had we not been, earth were still Eden. And people would live forever, would never know famine, suffering, loss, fear, pain—in short, they would not be human. Nor would there be progress upon the earth, for out of man's physical miseries, out of many tragic deaths, come the great discoveries of science, out of suffering and pain come strength and character.

Take the fields that once grew food for man's nourishment and then ceased to do so. Why? Because, for one reason, there was erosion—the trees cut down, the rain running off. And why was there erosion? Because of man's greed. He wanted to pasture more cattle or more sheep, he wanted to grow—and sell—more.

Only through mistakes and anguish can we grow, only through man's will and his drive to conquer ignorance does the world become a better place. It is a long process. And as long as greed, ambition, and ruthlessness remain, there will be wars. Someday, when the world wearies of destroying itself, the lesson will be learned.

Why, people demand, does God, all-powerful, permit the destructive storm, the typhoon and hurricane, the tidal wave and earthquake, the blizzard and avalanche, with their attendant loss of innocent life and property? When this little world was created it became subject to natural laws: the star, obeying its course; the moon and the sun influencing the tides, the great winds blowing, not idly, but according to their natures; the shaping and reshaping of earth as countless centuries pass.

Again people ask, why the tragic accidents: the overturned car that robs a family of a good father, the exploding stove that takes the lives of children, the escaping gas, the apartment fire?

But the car overturned, not because God looked in a book and said, *This car must be destroyed*, but because a driver was careless or because of a faulty mechanism, which can be traced only to faulty machines and hence back to the human element. And the stove exploded because of human carelessness, either before it was installed in that particular kitchen or afterward. Nothing "accidental" occurs which hasn't roots in the human element, nothing catastrophic occurs in Nature which has not roots in *her* laws.

It is often said that most of us waste God's time, and our own, by foolish prayer, the prayer of selfish petition. I don't think any prayer is foolish. The child who prays for a clear day for a picnic does not know, and would not understand if he knew, that if it does rain the disappointment was not sent to hurt him personally. It wasn't "sent" at all. It came because of the weather conditions, perhaps because of a disturbance which began a week before in another part of the country. As to wasting God's time, why, He has all the time there is or ever will be. And we certainly don't waste our own, for any turning to God, however trivial the reason, is something gained, whether or not the prayer be "answered."

And what is the answer, anyway? It is, I think,

often exactly opposed to that for which we have asked, yet still the answer.

I could pray until world's end for a million dollars —and I wouldn't acquire it, would I? This is, I am certain, just as possible to God as everything else. But, to begin with, it's a Santa Claus sort of prayer. Do I expect to wake up and find money stacked in bundles on the doorstep? I am sufficiently intelligent not to expect that. Yet suppose I have so prayed. Perhaps, at the end of my life, if I cast up the books I shall find that I have earned a million dollars—not all at once, and certainly keeping very little of it. Perhaps it wouldn't all be in dollars either but in things worth much more: friendships, growing abilities to perceive and treasure beauty, kindnesses when least expected—and opportunities, oh, *more* than a million dollars' worth of those!

I have prayed and been answered, perhaps in ways I never dreamed of. Rarely has it been the easy answer, usually it was an answer which meant I had to roll up my actual or spiritual sleeves and work it out for myself. But, as long as I worked it out, wasn't the prayer answered?

I find that I am after all a praying woman, sometimes, indeed most times, quite unconsciously and not in words. I don't suppose I ever sit down to the typewriter without prayer, without thinking, *God, help me to do a day's work.* I am currently engaged in writing a very difficult book; I dare say I pray when I begin my morning's work and when by nightfall it is ended. Often convinced that I can't go on, certain that I am hopelessly bogged down, I have stopped and asked for help, asked for the ability to find the right word or phrase.

There are, then, times when in a sense I, too, pray for a clear day for the picnic. If listening on a bad winter's night, when the roads are treacherous with ice, I pray that the child who has gone out in his car will soon be home, and then I hear wheels in the driveway, am I not justified in saying, *Thank God?* But, the skeptic says, the car must have been almost home before the prayer—and why should this particular car reach the garage safely and half a dozen other cars be wrecked?

The answer isn't far away. Of course the car was nearly home, but the prayer began before it left the garage, when I looked from the window and saw the storm. And the driver of the car is a careful one. He is not given to drowsiness on the road, nor to speeding, nor to drinking or discourtesy. The safety factors were always on his side—and prayed over, long before this one night.

I see no reason why we shouldn't appeal to God even in matters which seem trivial to onlookers. I misplace my glasses, without which I can't work, and find myself saying urgently, *Dear God, help me find my glasses.* If I put my hand on them immediately thereafter, I am grateful. I don't stop to inform myself they were there all the time. I know they were. But I didn't see them, did I?

Look at it this way. Those of us fortunate enough to have a good, wise father went to him with everything, however small or childish: the hurt, the bruise, the dawning knowledge of injustice, the adult difficulty. We asked for and obtained advice (not that we always followed it). And certainly, particularly as children, we besieged him—or our mother—with demands, requests: the toy we couldn't live without, the bike, the pony, the grown-up dress, the increased allowance—oh, a thousand and one things. Some of these he gave to us, and some he did not. And after a while we saw, perhaps through tears, why some of the things had not been forthcoming.

Sometimes it was because of a human limitation. Father couldn't afford the pony or the car or the increased allowance. We had to adjust to that. And perhaps at a later time the gift materialized. The pony became a horse which, because we were earning money, we were able to buy; the same was true of the car or the spending money. But why were we able to earn them? Because our parents had given us the ability—through heredity and through education.

I believe it is necessary to be grateful, both before and after the fulfillment of prayer; even when, for the time being, the prayer seems to go unanswered.

I know that I find myself, without conscious plan, thanking God a hundred times a day—not only for the glasses found, the letter received, the telephone ringing, but for the things we take for granted. That's a phrase to think about; for they are, you know, just that—*granted.*

Why shouldn't I thank Him for the sun streaming in through the south windows, for the leafing bough and the bursting bud, for sleep and food and friends, for the companionship of books, for human love which is but a reflection of His own? In short, for every good thing, and for the lessons which seem hard at the time but which, in the long view, help to pass a self-examination.

I am not afraid to importune God with my needs and desires. If they are right for me, He will show me the way to work them out, for my good and the good of others. If they aren't, well, how many times have I asked my mortal father for something that wasn't good for me? He, too, said no. No intelligent person can expect God to answer prayer which would work toward harm.

And if through our own powerful will, and quite without God's direction, we manage to drive our will through to another's detriment or to our own, we pay for it a hundredfold.

Easter, the springtime, comes back to the world, an answer to prayer. But as the date of the Easter season varies, the beginning of spring also varies. Did you ever stop to think that when we are knee-deep in autumn in this part of the globe it is elsewhere spring?

I thank God, always, that I am seeing another Easter season. Sometimes I have seen it dimly, sometimes with sorrow in my heart, sometimes with little personal hope. Yet, however I may feel, I must rejoice. Because now the dawn breaks after the winter night, and the great timeless story is unfolded in bud and springing grass before my eyes. This spring, as every spring, I am a praying woman.

MAY

1. ❀ *May Is for Remembering*

May, which brings us Spring at her sweetest, also ushers in Memorial Day—a meditative occasion for recalling those, both known and unknown to us, who have gone on before. Memorial, Decoration, or Confederate Day—depending on the state in which you live—was first established to honor those who fell in battle during the War Between the States. Of late it has also become a day on which to remember our civilian dead. Families which rarely betook themselves to a cemetery for a few moments of contemplation now turn out in full force for this solemn occasion.

I do not feel, however, that there should be only one day on which our dead are recalled. And I think our remembering should extend beyond our memories of those who have gone on before. For me Memorial Day is more than a commemoration—more even than a remembrance of heroic men who died for their convictions—it is a recalling of suffering and defeat as well as of victory.

We are told nowadays to forget our personal errors, erase our mistakes, expunge the past, and go forward. Basically that is good psychological therapy. No one can master himself if he sits and broods upon his past shortcomings, his failures, his sins. That way you learn nothing, for you never turn the next page of the book. But I do not believe that the errors, the sins, the wrong turn in the road should be *wholly* erased. I feel that all difficulties, troubles, and griefs should be remembered, but in this light: What have I done about it? How deeply have I repented? What progress have I made in my reparation? How much have I learned from my mistakes—and my sorrows?

This is facing up to reality, for what might have happened ten, twenty, or even forty years ago is still reality, and all that we remember is still true, however softened, idealized, or condoned it may have become by time.

If you were constituted so that everything that

happened to you was written on your mind, heart, and spirit in disappearing ink you would not be a particularly worth-while person. Character cannot be built with tissue paper that dissolves under the first shower. It has to be built of brick and steel—even though some of these materials may have flaws. Remember the stone the builders rejected? The 118th Psalm puts it simply: "The stone which the builders refused is become the head stone of the corner." The stones you refuse—the weight of sin, of error, the heavy shape of sorrow, the rough and irregular form of something left undone and now shot through with regret—all these, instead of being bitterly tossed aside, can be reshaped into an enduring strength. For it is from problems that we reach solutions, from mistakes that we gain knowledge, from sorrow that we achieve understanding.

How often have I heard people say of grief and disappointment, "I simply must forget it." Unless the disappointment is slight or the sorrow superficial, how can you forget? And even if you can I don't think you should. The memory of disappointment can be fashioned into a perhaps undreamed-of achievement. And the remembrance of sorrow can carry you deep into other burdened hearts and quicken your sympathy and understanding.

I suppose, too, that most of us have experienced a rare moment when everything was so completely right, so wholly good, so close to perfection, that we thought, "I must hold fast to this—for it may never come again." Or if we thought it might come again we felt we could never recapture its original fervor. Perhaps we never do relive such a moment—yet if we but let it, it will come to us again, many, many times, just through remembering.

And so it also seems foolish, even wrong, to forget the happiness of the past, even though it is inextricably interwoven with the sorrow of the present. For the sorrow is but the reverse side of the coin. It seems to me shortsighted to forget the mistakes, the humiliations, the injustices that are part of every man's pattern. They are irrefutably there. They are part of the total fabric of one's life. So why not face them bravely—if not every day, then at least once a year? For as you build with faulty stones as well as with unblemished ones, so you construct your own pattern from all sorts of materials—gay, bright, glowing, drab and soiled—and even as you build you can learn from your own life pattern.

Character is the spiritual house in which you live. It's never a perfect house—certainly never in this world. There are uneven floors, dark and cramped rooms, with here a rotting beam and there a dislodged brick. It is not always a comfortable house, nor one of which you can be so proud that you can throw wide the front door and invite a passer-by to come in and go through the house with you. Character is also the clothing of the spirit, and here, too, the garment can be inadequate, threadbare, even downright shoddy. But floors can be leveled, rooms opened to light and air, constricting walls torn down for greater freedom, and beams and bricks replaced. As for the designing, you can pick out a flaw in the pattern and with the courage and suffering of humility you can rebuild it.

So, there is little doubt that remembering helps—if you remember what you once set out to be, what you are now, how far short you fell of your goal; if you remember a mistake and refashion it into a sturdy rung in your ladder; if you remember a profound sorrow until you finally see it as the reverse side of the greatest happiness you have known. For, had you never fallen short of your goal, what incentive would you have for still trying to reach it? If you had never made a mistake, how would you know to avoid the same pitfall when next you see it? And if you had never suffered a humiliation, how would you understand a fellow man's wounded spirit? And perhaps even more importantly, if you had never known sorrow, how could you know happiness?

So, on Memorial Day—and other days as well—let us all take time to remember.

2. ꕥ *The Grateful Spirit*

It is not yet June, the day is bleak and a northeast wind rings the bells on the gingko tree outside my study. They hang from a cord, the rusted bells that were once on a Christmas wreath. Last summer we hung them on the gingko tree, close to the house, just outside my study. All summer long we heard them singing in the wind. My bedroom is directly above the study and the tree grows high; lying in the summer dark I could hear a reassuring tinkle. In winter, with storm windows, and none open during the day, the sound came faintly, but it was there, a sweet small voice. All winter, too, the juncos and chickadees perched there briefly above the bells, for I was sufficiently astute to scatter seed beneath the tree, where, if snow came, it rarely remained.

In our climate June is usually a wonderful month: the days are warm, the nights still cool. The flowers bloom, the shrubs blaze with color, the grass grows too fast for the pace of the lawn mower. The leaves of the trees are fresh, of an ineffable green, not yet dusty and drooping. The birds are still singing wildly, and occupied with their domestic duties. It is the month of open doors and picnics, the month when students of all ages mark off the days on their calendars and dream of vacations. We all do, for most of us are bound to a desk of some sort. It is the month of calm seas, of bright moons, of larger-seeming stars, of brides.

Time was when I was perturbed by the vagaries of nature. But now I am content, for if today does not dawn fair, tomorrow will, or the next day, or the next. I can wait. I long ago came to the conclusion that if each month brought only traditional weather, if every holiday was fair, if there were no surprises, we would soon be surfeited with complacency. There would be nothing to look forward to and the days would be dull with routine—no astonishments would greet us upon waking, we would live in the climate of heaven, and even the weatherman would grow bored, for he'd always be right.

Disappointment is, perhaps, a salutary thing, a disciplinary measure—and not only in regard to the weather. For when one hope perishes another is born. There are few of us, thank God, who run out of hope; the human heart seems endowed with an inexhaustible store. We move on, after the first despair, with a renewed determination, and what may have been disappointment becomes, at a later date, a much greater triumph than we lost. One path is blocked; we try another and, struggling along it, often come upon an open road and an achievable goal of which we had not dreamed.

It takes a long time to accept disappointment, still longer to be grateful for it. Disappointment is every man's lot. Who among us has not known it, seldom or often, in varying degrees? Disappointment in our work, our friends, surroundings, fortunes; disappointment in (and for) children. But the son you hoped would be a financial success becomes a financial failure, yet the most successful husband and father you've ever known. The daughter you hoped would be a great singer gives up her beginning career to work with unhappy children, to teach, or to become a fine housewife. The great poems you dreamed of writing came out pale and mediocre on paper but sang in your heart, transformed your day-by-day living, and that of those around you. The gadget you invented was of no practical use, despite the time, money, and devotion you spent on it, but from the failed invention came the idea for one which did not fail. The perfect sermons you longed to preach, the sermons that would save innumerable souls, somehow never were written, but your influence in your parish was a living sermon and that's what people remembered you for, not spectacular oratory. The brilliant surgery you dreamed you would one day perform was not to be, but as an obscure, dedicated physician you became, within the circle of your endeavor, a great man, profoundly loved and respected.

I have heard people say of a bitter disappointment, "I shall never get over it." Probably not, if they put their minds to it and set their will against growth. For to get over it, I surmise, means to surmount, to rise above, and those of us who can find the will to rise above are fortunate.

Gratitude is a rare trait, and rewarding. If I could ask for the qualities I most admire, I think gratitude would head the list—gratitude and humility. Oh, courage, of course, strength, integrity—who does not long for and strive after these? But gratitude is seldom mentioned in our prayers. It isn't easy, at the end of a tiring day or after some especially bitter trial, to ask, "Lord, make me grateful."

I believe that one of the things we find hardest to endure is the quality of what we think is ingratitude in other people. (We rarely examine ourselves in that respect.) How often do you hear people say, "After all I've done for him—this is how he repays me!" Parents use this weapon against their children. King Lear made an enduring complaint: "How sharper than a serpent's tooth it is to have a thankless child!" But His Shakespearean Majesty allowed no gratitude toward Cordelia, his "thankless" child who loved him but could, or would, not embroider her protestations with enameled phrases.

It is well known that the feeling that one is under obligation to *be* grateful burdens the mind and breeds dislike. The debtor avoids the man who has answered his appeal, the object of kindness turns from the benefactor. It is so much easier to give than to receive. So difficult to say "Thank you"—and mean it. It is also more usual to blame God for our failures than to thank Him for our triumphs.

It is a hard lesson we must learn, that of love, not charity, the lesson of the left hand which is not to know what the right hand doeth. For it is written in Matthew, "Take heed that ye do not your alms before men, to be seen of them."

All through the New Testament is the warning,

yet also the promise of inheritance: kindness to the stranger, meat for the hungry, drink for those who thirst, clothing for the naked, compassion for the sick and imprisoned. "Inasmuch," Jesus said, "as ye have done it unto one of the least of these my brethren, ye have done it unto me."

But there is not a word about expecting gratitude from these least . . .

When we learn that whatever mercy, understanding, and assistance we furnish is, in reality, for Him, then we do not think of repayment, whether it be ill or good. But, someone might argue, Jesus also said, "Let your light so shine before men, that they may see your good works, and glorify your Father . . ."

Surely, He did not mean the bright, brief light of personal publicity, but the light of the spiritual man. This is not concentrated upon a single kindness nor upon multiple benevolences—it is a certain glory from within, steady, not transient, and never blinding. It is the light by which we recognize the good human being.

All last winter I pondered on gratitude. Every morning I cut up suet, broke bread and cake into crumbs, saved bits from the family table, bought seed. And went out, in rain or sun, in snow or sleet, and replenished the three tall feeders and scattered seed upon the ground in sheltered sites. If I was late, the birds sat huddled in shrub and tree branches and walked, scolding in thin, querulous voices. Sometimes they didn't appear at all until some hours had elapsed. But by next morning the suet was gone and the crumbs, and the seeds were empty hulls upon the ground. None, however, thanked me. They did not burst into unseasonable song at my approach. Rather, they fled.

This omission has not turned me against the birds. In their ordinary way of going about their feathered business there is reward and to spare; they are not chirping for me on cold winter mornings nor displaying, only for me, a pattern of wings against a dreary sky; they do not nest nearby, in spring, in order to enchant me with bright coloring and wonderful song. All this they would do if I had not spared them so much as one crumb, one grain of sand when the snow covered the gravel, one drop of running water.

When, over the years, you have in small ways and large given of yourself to others, perhaps few will remember. It takes most of us a long time to accept this; some never do. But if this knowledge is reached, then you regret the stupid hurts, the unavailing anger, the bruised ego. You forget the curious pigeonholes into which you put people—one marked worthy, one unworthy, the white sheep, the black, the geese, and the swans. For who are you to judge? Have you walked in this man's shoes or seen into that man's heart?

I think that when we have said the Lord's Prayer we may humbly add one more petition. Daily we ask for bread, we ask that our debts be forgiven, that we be not led into temptation, that we be delivered from evil. All these things we ask, and expect, but we do not ask also, "Teach us to be truly grateful."

For this is the one gratitude owed, the only one.

So, with June knocking at the door, that spring-into-summer month which for a year we have not seen, shall we not be grateful for the season, whatever it brings, for each other, for the disappointment as well as the hope, for the postponement as well as the fulfillment? All come from God.

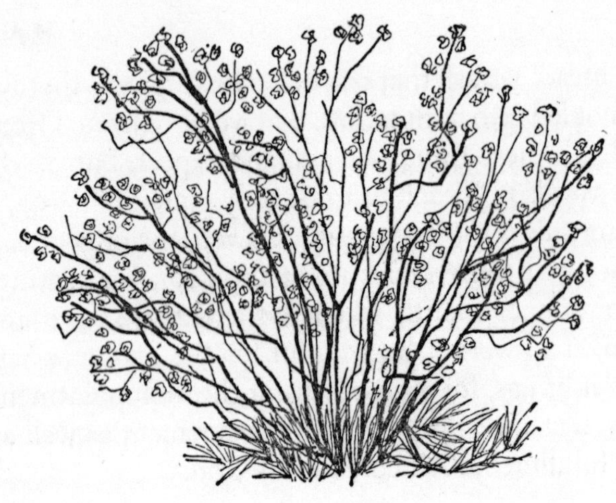

JUNE

1. ❀ *Blossoms, Brides, and Blizzards*

It seems to me that Nature in spring is like a spendthrift aunt who is suddenly overtaken by an irresistible urge for generosity. She gives with both hands, with the utmost lavishness, and then, as if fearful that her bank account will be overdrawn, has a complete change of heart and settles down to a season of thrift.

I am not discounting the summer gardens, but am thinking mainly of the spring flowers, which appear almost simultaneously in our section of the world. The bulb flower has scarcely been admired when trees and bushes burst into bloom. Lilacs are laden, dogwood is white or rosy snow, orchards are a drift of beauty. What with one thing and another, wild or cultivated, it is a season almost too lovely to bear. Your heart runs from one beauty to another.

My birthday is in October. A few years ago my sister bought me a present, a gift which was delivered in April! It appears that the Brooklyn Botanical Gardens have developed a weeping flowering crab tree. They have now issued what they call a limited edition of one thousand trees for sale. Mine is number 301. It has been planted so that we can see it from the big south window. In blossomtime it produces white flowers of no special significance. But in the autumn the fruit is superb and cascades red along the drooping boughs. It is called Red Jade, and since April it has been the center of interest. First the arrival and the planting, then the wondering if it would flower, and now the looking ahead to summer's end and scarlet fruit.

Looking ahead is what keeps anyone spiritually alive. Still I wish that the spring flowering of shrub and tree could extend into summer. Summer brings no flowering trees except the Rose of Sharon and the catalpa. Our Rose of Sharon is a neglected shrub; it must be very old. As for the catalpa, it was cut down by the wind and ice this past season.

But Nature's way, which is God's, is the right way. Brief spring and gorgeous flower, and then the green leaf and the slow building of fruit for man or bird.

There is nothing to do but wait for the breaking bloom, enjoy it for as long as it lasts, and go with the season into the lazy depths of summer and wait again for the appearance of the fruit and the bounteous harvest.

This month, June, is traditionally the month of brides, which seems quite fitting—a stepping from spring into early summer. In our family, tradition has not always held. I was married in November, and before Christmas I sailed away into a subtropical country, hence also, into summer.

My older daughter selected June for her wedding. I recall it as one of the loveliest days I have ever known, neither too warm nor too chill. She was married in the chapel of her school some miles distant. She chose her own music, which was beautiful. There were present in the little chapel only members of her family and the family of the boy she married, and a few people from the school, which was closed for the summer. Some of the day pupils lived nearby and came in their little white robes to ring the chapel bells and light the candles. This is the chapel where the school worships night and morning. The rafters bear in faded gold the names of the graduates. It is a very small structure, standing apart, and on this day we left the doors wide open. During the ceremony I could hear the birds singing.

My older son was married in a big church in September. That, too, was a small wedding, and there was a sharp bite in the clear evening air. One January not too long ago my only niece was married, also in the city. It was a cold, windy, clear day. This was a very big church wedding, and the bride, a very little girl, was just past eighteen. The flower girl, who was five, looked enough like her to be her sister instead of her niece.

That, too, was a beautiful wedding and it occurred to me that, June or January, every month is a bride's month. All weddings are lovely and each bride is more beautiful than the last.

Recently I was on a television panel which occasionally I invade. It is an interesting one, for upon it five generations are represented. The same questions are asked of us all, and we must answer them. The varying viewpoints are, I think, of some significance. The youngest panel member can be anywhere from seven to nine, the oldest from eighty to ninety. It is sobering to reflect, after sitting in a time or two, that only the very young and the very old seem to see things as black or white, with no intermediate shades, and are able to answer with a simple unqualified "yes" or "no." Those of us in the middle groups are much more likely to say "if," "or," "but," "perhaps," or "maybe."

One of the questions asked was what advice each of us would give a young couple about to be married. Television time is valuable and the answers, however spontaneous, have to be brief. There are five of us to reply and, if time permits, to argue among ourselves. I dare say I could have gone on for hours advising a prospective bride and groom.

As I recall my scant reply, it was to the effect that a happy marriage has to be built. This is hardly a new idea. We all know that the foundation is, or should be, love. But sometimes we don't know our building materials. I said, and believe, that you build not a house, but a fortress. It's slow work. Some of the material you may already possess, if you're lucky. Some you have to create. And, I dare say, the principal ingredients are trust, loyalty, patience, and a leaven of humor.

Now that I am able to enlarge upon the subject in this month of brides, I would add as an ingredient unselfishness, also having much in common. This doesn't necessarily mean cultural tastes. I know happy folks who like very different cultural things. Let us say, he likes modern music and she prefers classics. Or he likes mysteries and she enjoys biography or historical romances. He is charmed by art, in any form, and she is not. You could go on making lists indefinitely. These differences of personal taste loom large sometimes but can be easily resolved if each is willing to concede to the other, and even try to understand.

If an engaged couple seeks advice, it is too late to tell them that an approximately similar education and background is helpful in marriage. They are already engaged and cannot alter their original environments and opportunities. Absolutely essential, I believe, to a happy marriage is firm religious faith. Thousands of people have, of course, found that they, in their little household, are alone in their belief in God. But those who know that it is shared, and who together turn to the Source of all aid and consolation, are building a fortress that will be impregnable.

All this I would tell the imaginary young couple, knowing that, in common with us all, they must work out their own problems.

So, now in June, happy is the bride the sun shines on; even if it rains, happy is the bride.

You may be wondering what blizzards have to do with brides and blossoms. Nothing, of course. June is not the month for unusual belated snow. But this particular spring reminds me of blizzards and other unpleasant manifestations of climate. As I have said before, scars are soon covered by the leafing of branches. If you look closely you see that some branches are no longer there and that despite its brave show a tree is maimed. Here and there are stumps to remind us of something forever lost, something which took ten, twenty, fifty, or even a hundred years to grow. Then in a single night, or a moment, it was gone—like man himself.

Looking back, I reflect with gratitude on the little gasoline-operated generator in the cellar. This was installed when we moved, aware that our artesian water was pumped direct, and that we had only one furnace, an oil burner. In the former house we had a thousand-gallon tank for water storage, and a second furnace, which burned coal. Two women alone lead a precarious sort of existence in stormy weather, so in went the generator. It works like an outboard motor, with a cord to start it humming; it is, I might say, a busy, noisy little gadget. But it's a noise you like to hear when all public utilities are shut off, and you know you have heat, water, refrigeration, and even emergency lights.

I recall sitting by the window listening to the hum in the dark, for I didn't need light at the moment. Suddenly the lights came on, one by one in the other houses. I realized that the power was on, and our generator could be silenced again. It was an eerie sensation to watch the light appear. Some people had had their porch lights on when, forty-eight hours earlier, the power had been shut off. Now they appeared again, as brave a sight as you could imagine.

Those of us who had generators were fortunate, and in our situation, with a very bad case of flu in the house, we were doubly so. I couldn't hold with those people who cried what fun it was to huddle together in one room over an oil stove, cook on an open fireplace, and read by lamplight. I have absolutely no desire to become a pioneer! My younger son, mercifully home that week end and an efficient generator-sitter, infuriated me by inquiring if I didn't recall the pioneer days. I replied that I had not come over on the *Mayflower* nor ever trekked across our land via covered wagon. He also refers to my girlhood as "the olden days," a term which makes me think of King Arthur and the Round Table.

But the generator, during the time it functioned and now every month when it is checked and turned over, set me thinking about matters not associated with the common blessings of light, heat, and water. Each of us has, at his command, a generator which functions, if we call upon it, in time of darkness. None escapes black hours, whether they be caused by fear, anxiety, grief, regret, or frustration—hours not only of darkness but of bitter cold, though the calendar may stand at June. You know the kind of cold I mean. It can even be communicated physically to the person experiencing it, a deadly chill creeping upward to the heart.

This generator is, of course, faith. It is prayer. Many of us have learned to rely upon it in good times as well as in bad, in the everyday course of living. It is there to reinforce our power of courage and hope. In bad times it *generates*. Everything may appear lost and hopeless. We haven't an ounce of courage with which to press onward nor a ray of hope to warm the shivering heart. But once we manage to start the generator warmth flows back and with it comes all the courage we need.

June or January, year round, each of us possesses this marvelous source of strength. Some have learned more easily how to draw upon it. Others come to knowledge slowly and painfully. But it is there, no matter what has fallen or betides—whether a crisis in the private domestic circle or one which threatens all mankind.

The sorrows of men are multiple. Disaster comes in the night, sometimes through a man's own deed, sometimes falling upon the guiltless. The hidden strength is geared to function in any emergency. I believe that, like the mechanical generator in my cellar, it should be kept in use, turned over, as the phrase goes, in time of smooth going. The impulse to pray is not one which should be kept for Sundays or time of trouble. It is an everyday tonic and strengthener. Like any faculty, whether of imagination or of muscle, it grows stronger with exercise. Then, when darkness falls and the lethal cold begins to claw with icy fingers at the frightened heart, it is so easy to start the all-powerful engine and feel hope and courage flowing back again.

Reliance upon prayer and a turning to God is not a matter of the calendar nor of the immediate situation. It is always. It is forever. *It is now.*

2. *Silver Platters*

Recently I have been delving into what are known in the publishing business as "How To" books. Most volumes of this sort are concerned with instructing the reader in such matters as how to build a house, how to raise children, or how to sail a boat. The books I have been reading, however, tell a reader how to find peace and contentment and possibly some degree of spiritual development.

This is a subject I have been reading for years. I recall that once, when I was very young, I took a course in yoga—a system of mental and physical disciplines developed in India. I didn't get far with it. Having to hold my breath for long periods of time made me dizzy, and when I attempted the exercise on concentration my mind wandered all over the place. I am one of those unfortunates who simply must learn things all by myself—the hard way. This has been true even of my writing. There are any number of valuable books on writing technique, and many of my friends have benefited from them. But not me. Trial and error, rejection and revision, have been my only effective, if often heartless, teachers.

And now I find I have had exactly the same experience with instructions on how to achieve mental and spiritual serenity. Some of these books are almost entirely psychological, others combine psychology with religious concepts. Many have a Pollyanna approach that is all sweetness and light. Others strive to wrestle realistically with life. As a young girl I read these books with starry-eyed expectancy. As a young woman I read them with mental reservations.

Now I read them and sigh. It's the old story. I can learn only from my own stumbling, fumbling experience.

I am aware that basic truths are often contained in these books. Many are written by extremely competent authors—distinguished clergymen, scholarly laymen, skilled scientists. Frequently their theories are based on time-tested philosophies and psychological techniques. But some of these books also assure their readers that if they diligently practice the methods recommended they will be able to conquer practically every problem known to mankind—including poverty, bad digestion, and being unappreciated by the boss. I don't doubt that for certain people these books may be able to do what they claim. When a friend tells me excitedly, "You must read the book I just bought—it has helped me tremendously," I feel sure that it has, and I am happy for her. But when I read the volume, sometimes I find it doesn't help me at all. At best it merely presents a truth which, by means of bruising and head-battering experience, I have somehow managed to learn by myself.

There is, however, one thing about these books which exasperates me. Practically none of them ever stresses the fact that before you can get something worth while you have to work for it. Most of them seem to suggest that you have to do just one thing—aim your thoughts at what you want. I am well aware of the effectiveness of concentrated thought. But I do not believe for a moment that you can shoot your thoughts out like arrows and then have your objective drop neatly into your lap like an overripe plum. However, there are a lot of people who do believe that. For half an hour they give themselves over to plain and fancy masterminding—and then, exhausted, they sit back and wait for the knock at the door that will signify the arrival of the proverbial silver platter groaningly loaded with health, wealth, and happiness. Or, as we used to say, "They look for pie in the sky."

I am not suggesting that there is anything wrong with dreaming, hoping, or even wishful thinking. I do a lot of all three myself. But I find that before I get what I want I also have to work hard for it. And part of that work—perhaps the most difficult part—is my fight to hold off the doubts, fears, and discouragement that threaten to overwhelm me. I know few people who are as anxiety-ridden and as easily discouraged as I am. Through the years I have learned to do something about these problems. But not through any book I have read—with one outstanding exception. It is the Bible, the Book that has given us our greatest insights and profoundest wisdoms, such as "For as he thinketh in his heart, so is he" . . . "Ask, and it shall be given you" . . . "Seek, and ye shall find."

In the parable of the "talents" (which in Biblical

times were units of money, as well as personal abilities) Jesus praised those who used their talents to good advantage and decried those who buried their talents and waited for minor miracles to descend from heaven. As a monetary unit a talent does little good hidden under a mattress. As a personal ability it has equally little merit if it is never employed. In my own profession I have had hundreds of people tell me that they would be gifted writers "if only I had the time." Or their first rejection slip comes to them as such an outrageous affront that they promptly abandon their typewriters and spend the rest of their lives boring their friends with the explanation that if they had the opportunity and the "inside influence" they could write a novel which would bring them the fame and fortune their talent deserves. Possibly they do have talent, but they bury it under a mass of excuse and procrastination. Or, what I find even more incredible, they say, with a tone of magical wonder in their voices, "If only I could find the inspiration"—as if inspiration meant that you could put a clean sheet of paper into a typewriter, go to bed, get up the next morning, and lo, there on the paper, all by itself, would be the greatest sonnet of all time.

Unfortunately—or perhaps I should say, fortunately—writing doesn't evolve that way. Nor does anything else. God equipped each of us with ability of one sort or another. But I don't think He ever intended that our ability should work for us unless we also work for it. A talent is a kind of emotional muscle. It must be constantly exercised. Ignore it and it will atrophy.

There are many books which tell us we must love our fellow man. But they don't tell us *how*—very probably because no one can tell us how. Certainly no one can explain how you can love someone you don't even like, or who perhaps has even wronged you. The most anyone can tell you is that you should put angry and vindictive thoughts out of your mind and replace them with thoughts of love and kindness. And this is not so easy as it sounds, because primarily it is a job of merciless self-searching. Why *don't* you like Mrs. Jones? Is it because of her manner, or because she is opinionated, or because she has a fine home and travels in more elegant circles? And as for Mr. Smith who, you feel, has gratuitously wronged you—is he completely to blame or were you also at fault? Could it be because of some wrong you once did him?

Sincerely trying to find the truth takes courage and, if you are able to find it, it may well leave you feeling uncomfortable or even ashamed. Yet this honest facing of the truth may be the beginning of a priceless habit in which you will *always* honestly face yourself and those about you. In your new honesty it may be that you will find something to admire in Mrs. Jones, even if it is only her pleasant voice or the lighthearted way she has of walking down the street. And the same can be said of Mr. Smith, if it is based solely upon the fact that he seems unaware of your hostility toward him. In both cases, *you* have the final decision—friendship or futility.

JULY

1. ❀ *Turn in the Road*

I remember one year, not long ago, when I listened to the singing of the birds and thought with horror and astonishment, for the first time in my life, "I cannot welcome spring." This was true. Rather, I resented it. Mine was a winter mood, the mood of a New England winter, bare, zero-cold, unrelenting. I had liked the early darkness, the falling of barometer and temperature, the screaming wind—although normally I am adverse to a wind which screams—the drifts and falling snow. These gave me ample excuse not to go out, but to sit—usually idle—at my desk or by a hearth fire, with a cup of tea beside me and a book in my hand. I regretted when the thaws came and the warm wind. I had no joy in the courageous flower beneath the last light snow, which we call "sugar snow," nor in the branch, suddenly alive with sap, not even in the fragile returning green, the budding fruit tree. The seasons swung, the wheel turned, but I wanted to stay where I'd been for a long time, static, in the middle of a bitter, icy winter. The heart knows its own climate.

The reasons for my resentment are of no moment. All of us have different, and to us sound, reasons when we refuse or wish to refuse to accept change, however familiar and recurrent. As a matter of fact, many of my reasons still remain problems, practical or emotional, as yet unsolved. But I have learned to go along with the seasons.

That was the April I walked in our own fields, surprising wild animals, flushing birds, watching the brook, brimmed with recent rains, run free and brown, over sand and stone, in the woods. The April wind was sweet and chill, the sun warm. I knew then that the time must come when I must leave these acres, and the house beyond the fields and woods, the rugged pattern of old stone walls . . . I was sad not only because I expected soon to leave this treasured home but because of changing times, and alterations in our lives; common sense dictated that the acres were too many, the upkeep too hard, the house far too big for a greatly reduced family.

On that April day, I tried to *accept.* Of the flowering shrubs and fruit trees planted since we came here, the majority had been gifts from family or friends. The hedge was of our planting, the dogwoods, and all but three of the forty-six lilacs. I know who gave me the hawthorns, the laburnum, the shad bush, the ornamental crab apple, cherry, and plum. And who brought the holly tree to stand by the terrace. I know whose thought it was to make the big beds of valley lilies, and who sent the standing roses. To leave them would be leaving people I love.

I have ties even with the destructive red fox who, every year, brings his mate to a field nearby and probably usurps, and enlarges, a woodchuck hole. The fox, the vixen, and the babies they raise sometimes come out to frolic and to bark, late afternoons. I am familiar with pheasant, their rusty cry and the sound their fledglings make. I am aware of where the deer lie down in a magic circle, in the fields . . . I have seen them, close to the house, at dawn or sunset, standing quite still. In this state they are protected, and come to the back of the garage to feed, in autumn, on the fallen apples. During severe winters we put food in pheasant shelters, for we do not allow the land to be shot over, and even hay for the deer. As for the returning birds, we watch for the tanager, the oriole, both Baltimore and orchard, the kingbirds, the robin and bluebird, and all the others. Those which linger over cold months are fed—and joined by birds often alien to this section. I have often seen bluebirds in the holly berries, robins flying over snow. But it is to those which year in year out return to a known tree that I am most deeply attached.

You may say, "But if you go elsewhere in the country, there will be other birds, other trees and shrubs and gardens, other voices to speak in the night, the bark of a fox, the cry of a drowsy bird, the hoot of an owl." This, of course, is true, but always I have the feeling that it is getting late to begin again.

My younger daughter, then at home for just a little while longer, had picked up a catch phrase from somewhere. Every now and again I would hear her clear young voice, raised in mock anger or dismay, "How too revolting!" from upstairs or the kitchen or outdoors. I was not in the least alarmed. I was certain that she had broken a finger nail, dialed a wrong number, broken a dish, forgotten a butter spreader or the coffee pot, or out walking stepped into a puddle. But that April day I could easily echo her plaint. "How too revolting," I could say and then go on to amplify, "how cruel, how incredible, how beyond thinking!"

We have lived here over a decade. This is not much time out of a life, but it has been the good time in many ways. Rebuilding a house into a home, setting out bush and tree, watching them grow from silly little sticks into sturdy beauty, this is a satisfying task of the heart. Many of our pine trees were once hung with bright ornaments; given us by a friend each Christmas, they were living and, after the New Year, we planted them. How they grew! We lost one, an early one, in our last big blow; it was a foot around and forty feet high.

To leave a home, even to contemplate leaving, is a special sort of wrenching agony. Here your children have, like the trees, grown, here you have experienced delight, sorrow, or anxiety until it has become part of the walls; here you have slept peacefully or lain awake wondering. And here your friends have come, in good times and bad, and sat with you a little while. It has all soaked in . . . it has taken root.

A year or so ago, I suffered a sort of spiritual sea change. It was when a member of my household sent to an upstate nursery for two apple trees, special trees, each bearing five kinds of apples. One she planted on a neighbor's property, the other in a place near our cherry tree which had come to us, a mere stick, like this new apple tree, and now brings blossoms, shade, and fruit each year.

I thought, but did not say, "What's the use? If we must leave, so be it; it will be some years before the five kinds of apples make their astonishing appearance, and we'll not be here to see, and gather, them."

After the big storm, Thanksgiving time, I walked

down to see how the newcomer had fared. It stood, as did most of our other trees. It was small and bare, it had offered no resistance to the wind.

. . And it came to me that I, too, would offer no resistance to the winds of change; I also would stand, however transplanted.

And I said to myself, "If I must go away, someone else will enjoy the new tree; meantime, it is here for me to enjoy."

Perhaps that is true philosophy, to enjoy, and be grateful for, that which you know you have, and if it is taken from you, to remember, holding it forever in your heart, where it cannot be lost.

The April wind will sing through the quickening branch again, the birds return, the great, recurrent preoccupation with life, the resurrection of life begins again its cycle. And I think, wherever we go, there will be roots, there will be seasons, there will be a house to make into a home. The children will return, wherever we are, for surely they are as faithful as the birds that visit us.

None living can foresee the future . . . none of us can know whether we go or stay, in the restricted sense or in the larger. No one is sure of anything in this dark, perilous time, except that it will be spring again, that one season follows upon another, that the stars will shine, the moon rise, and the sun . . . and that we have love, friendship, and companionship. Of these things we are certain; and, over and above that certainty, we are sure of God's unfailing love, and of His strength, the eternal Source, which is always there for us to draw upon. It cannot be taken from us nor lost, it is merely that we forget, so often, to use it.

I believe that it was meant that we enjoy these durable blessings, which cannot be destroyed; and also, those not so durable, which have been lent to us for a while. They are our own, for any one of a number of reasons: we have worked for and earned them, or they have come about through circumstance, or by sheer good fortune. Because the world is uneasy, and sorrow and grief and fear eat into the fibers like cancer, we need not hold remote the everyday gifts: the sunset beyond the window, the woods, speaking as we walk, the bright wing in flight. We need not shut ourselves away from laughter, or the homely enjoyments: a cup of tea shared with a friend, the smell of cookies baking, the sound of music, the doors a fine book opens to us—the thousand and one innocent pleasures which have become part of the life pattern.

Into the unforeseeable future we can take all this, and the good memories. We can take whatever work we are destined to accomplish, for as long as we are enabled to work. Wherever we go and whatever we may do, the love of family and friends goes with us, part of the great abiding love of God, as the many streams and rivers and the least drop of rain are all part of the sea.

I have stopped being sorry for myself, and fearful of change. But now and then the most absurd anxieties pierce me, like a pin thrust. How can I sort and pack, for keeping and giving, four thousand books? Will the painting especially painted for the long narrow space over the living-room mantel fit into any other house? And what about the curtains, the material bought in Honolulu many years ago? Any woman will understand this; a man will shake his head in tolerance and wonder at the infinite capacity of womenfolk for worrying about nonessentials.

It all smooths out to this: Whatever comes will come; and in this particular situation, surely for the best. Leaving a home you cherish is loss. But relative, proportionate. It is not loss of life, your own or another's; it is not illness; it is not the end of the world you know; it's only the end of part of it. For when one door closes another must open. This is the promise implicit in the April wind: the door of winter shuts, the spring door opens; beyond spring, the full summer, past summer, the brilliant falling leaves, then, the cycle nearing completion, winter again.

To the Christian spirit, spring is the pledge of the risen Christ. I who have been sorrowful in springtime know that the earth's renaissance can be hard to bear. And all over this dismayed, fearing, grieving world there are numberless who face the spring with painful reluctance. Yet the promise is still in the April wind, the symbol of hope and renewal. After hope and renewal, courage must follow, for these are woven of the same fabric.

Lift up your hearts, for beyond the temporal springtime there is Life Everlasting.

Now that we have sold the house, we must move on. As I write, the preliminaries are ten days beyond me. Soon, when the summer heat sets down upon this part of the world, we'll be gone. We have found no place which, as you enter, says quietly, "This could be home." I have been told that the buyer must never permit himself to be panicked; but that's easier said than done.

We have looked from here to there and back again; tramped land, climbed stairs, descended into cellars, ascended to attics, peered into clothes closets, asked a million questions. Out of twenty houses or more, we have seen two we liked; each had strings to it, disadvantages which could weave into ropes with which to hang your hopes. There is still time, they tell me.

When we moved here from the city we had no preconceived notions. We simply wanted *out*—out into the country. We didn't like the city house; we left it without a qualm. As for the place we bought, the Victorian, somewhat remodeled farmhouse, and twenty-five lovely acres, trees, stone walls, views to the ridge, brooks, laurel—well, we saw it three times and fell in love. Naïve, innocent, we had no thought for its disintegrating innards, for the million and one repairs and rebuilding into which we would have to pour energy, intelligence, and money. But gradually —even after the twenty-two workmen who invaded us that first summer and autumn had gone—we built it around us, for comfort and satisfaction. There were four children then; we sent them away for the summer of building and they returned to their new home, new friends, new schools, with great excitement. Their ages ranged from thirteen to nine. We did not stop to think that they'd change—we forget the inevitability of growth, boarding school, college, marriage—and the thought of war never occurred to us.

By the time we leave this place, the last two will have gone, one to the West to live and work and the other to a waiting job or back into the Navy. As for the older children, married and away, they are distant.

So now we will be two women in an enormous house. And we know how sensible we are to sell; how fortunate to find a buyer with five children who needs space!

The mind is convinced but the heart is stubborn. The roots go deep, you dig them out, they bleed and are wrenched.

Everything in this house speaks to us of planning, of sacrifice, of friends. Outdoors it is as familiar as one's hand; we have done the planting, except for the century-old trees and a few shrubs. The tall firs were once living Christmas trees, in the house for a bright, lovely season, and then planted outside, to continue their lives. Two have *twice* been Christmas trees; when failing to find what we wished, we cut from their tall tops and left them to recover—which they did. And all were given us. Given us, too, were the dogwoods, hawthorn, flowering crabs and cherries—and one member of the family counted the lilacs last year and found we had forty-six. There were three or four on the place when we came. There isn't a blossom, come spring, that I cannot call by the name of the giver.

The standing roses are rather new—twice they have bloomed—a gift. But the wonderful climbers were brought here from the city so long ago. The huge beds of valley lilies began with a gift to me. The peonies were brought from Ohio by the people who owned the house before us.

Am I foolish to weep inwardly over the birds? In winter they come to the feeders—some every year, some as exciting rare visitors. In summer the same birds return to build—the orchard and Baltimore orioles, the bluebirds and kingbirds, the robins and wrens, the bobolinks, the scarlet tanagers. One day they aren't there; the next, we watch a wild bright flight. One spring morning I waken to the chorus in the ancient apple tree beyond my bedroom windows, and walk to the garage after breakfast because I know the thrashers will be busy in the lilacs and the swallows will write their signature against the sky when dusk falls. And in the apple orchard that we planted, there will be countless wings. The wild azalea will bloom, and the laurel . . .

These past fifteen years were good. This house has character because much has happened in it. Built in 1854 by farm people, after the really old house was abandoned, it remained in the family long enough for three generations to be born in it; then it changed hands and within a few years came to us. Here we have known great happiness, productive work, the usual amount of anxiety, and problems everyone must meet. We have seen, from these doors, the two boys go off to war, and return; we have seen a girl in white walk down the path and step into the car that took her to the chapel where she was married. From this house they've gone to school, to parties, to college—and come home again.

For the adults these were the working years, years in which we traveled far and, happily, returned. I look at the walls and think of the sounds they've absorbed—laughter, weeping, the footsteps of family and friends, the clatter of the typewriter keys.

Now it seems late to begin again to make a home. For a home is more than shelter, more than rent or purchase price, more than an asset in a ledger. It is part of those who live in it, a beating heart. And no house is a home until it has been lived in, and molded, until it fits you somehow, like the shell fits the snail, like his armor the turtle. It must not close you in, remote from the world, and its suffering, its sharing, but unless it becomes a symbol of security and a friendly fortress, it is not a home.

Time runs out for those of us no longer young nor in our energetic middle age. Wherever we go, when we plant a shrub or a tree, as we will of course do, it must be a big one, for we cannot wait another fifteen years to see its full growth.

This house is permeated with prayer, with all the petitions that have gone beyond the walls—you know them well: the prayer for someone's safety, for someone's recovery from grave illness, the prayer for guidance, for help, the prayer that the eyes of the soul be opened to the everlasting promise that no wild petition is needed, for the Father knows and hears even before the words are spoken.

For some time I had told myself, "If it is right that we must go, then go we shall and at the fitting time." And it happened in just that way, in almost the twinkling of an eye. And now, all my waking moments, it seems, the mute appeal runs through the pattern of thinking, working, going about the daily tasks. "Let us find the place which is right for us. Because somewhere such a place must exist and we must be led to it, for the rest of our days. A smaller place, a house which will become a home, one to which the children can return, and in which no great burden, as here, will fall upon those who will there live out their lives."

I write, and the telephone sits beside me, black and mute. Then it rings, but so far no voice says, "I have found the place; you will be able to make it your own." I go off to conduct a class at a neighboring school on the rewards and obstacles integral to writing, and the family looks at houses with an agent. I return and wait for them, thinking they will erupt into the house crying, "We have seen it! It is what we want." That hasn't happened yet, either.

No—they come home, and their muscles ache from the in-and-out of cars, from the up-and-down of stairs; their minds are a little numb, they can scarcely remember all they have seen and inspected. This house becomes confused with that house, and where was the other one? But no matter; none is suitable.

Unfortunately, having lived in the country for fifteen years, we are no longer naïve, no longer innocent of possible pitfalls, of disadvantages. Nor are we geared to the noise, anxiety, and problems of rebuilding. We cannot cope with it; we refuse to do so. Now we are acquainted with mundane drawbacks, we inquire about roofs, cellars, water and heating systems. We look closely at proximity to main roads; we must be near one, but not too near. In our years in the country we have learned.

We have also learned that the advertisements that halo the unvisited house with promise, even glamour, can be factual and at the same time misleading.

Consider the accumulation of these years, to say nothing of the years before that. Consider some four thousand books. Consider the furniture we won't need but cannot discard until we know where we're going and what will fit into where! Consider all this, and the brain is staggered.

Everyone tells us how wise we are, how sensible, how fortunate. Our minds agree, but the foolish heart is not persuaded; the heart is like an old dog by a familiar fireside. It is frightened by strange country and voices. Banish it from its place by the fire, and it whimpers.

We have dear friends who have written us a letter. In the letter they say, in effect, that no one can buy or lease the house, in reality, nor can they drive us from it. It remains in the hearts of friends, as we remain. It is part of us; we take it, the essence of the home it has been, wherever we may go. Of all the words written or spoken in this hour these were the most comforting.

Common sense, reason, logic, the irrefutable arguments—these stand. I admit the two-and-two-makes-four truth. I admit the unreason of heartbreak. I admit the selfishness. With the world a little mad with terrible suffering, grief, uncertainty all about us; with, at any time in history, war or no war, inequalities, poverty, injustice, sorrow—how stupid, how immature, how nearly wicked to mourn over something built of wood, to grieve for tree and flower, for brook and bird! I stop to think of the world's displaced people, those who have lost not only homes but parents, friends, children, hope, and even identity. Where do they wander? Is there a place for them, when shall they reach it, and if they do, with what searing memories and unhealing wounds? I think of these, and am ashamed. How like one grain of sand in a desert is my unhappiness! I have lost nothing, but, of my own volition, have sold something. I can buy something else, can't I?

All this I understand, with this I am in agreement. My affliction is rooted in sentiment, emotion, ego, and perhaps fear. These roots, too, must be dug out, cast aside. For I am slowly winning my way to the place where I will know that God intends growth and change, alteration and adjustment. The road cannot run in a straight line from birth to death, from Now to Eternity, not for the world, the races, not for any one of us personally. None living remains infant, child, adolescent; the years are stopped for no one. The road turns and we turn with it, and if we are wise we do not look back. Those of us who cannot, with His help, adjust ourselves come, instead, to a very dark place. Life, growth, adjustment, light—these He intended for us. Waking, and before I sleep, and during the troubled, busy day, I tell myself this. For it is true. It is right that we move on, that once again young voices echo here, that others find happiness, security, and love within these walls, that life, in effect, begin again.

And, so, we shall come to a place, our own place, by what means I do not know, nor when. Here at my hand is the promise. I do not need to read it. I speak it to myself, in silence, many times a day . . .

"The Lord is my shepherd; I shall not want.

"He maketh me to lie down in green pastures; he leadeth me beside the still waters."

2. ❀ *Road's End—a Portrait of a House*

In July the part of the world in which I live stands knee-deep in summer. This is a section where wooded ridges march along the horizon, the roads curve and dip, climb and turn. Soon, in August, the trees will be heavy with foliage, the birds, except at dawn and dusk, will hide in the woods, the moon rises gold, and at practically any time of day or night lightning may flash and thunder roll like war drums. It will be hot in August here, and humid, but by nightfall, when the whippoorwill speaks, it's cool.

The year is already moving into this lazy month, heat is rising from the country roads, beaches are black with people, cars race past filled with holiday seekers—and soon we will have moved into a new home.

We found it shortly after I last wrote of sorrow and hope. We had looked in every direction, we had seen innumerable houses. Many had delightful features, some were utterly impossible; none was right. We saw one old house which appealed to us. It was five miles from a railroad station, which was a drawback; also, the price was too high. In a moment of madness we made an offer for it, came home to brood about it, and to awaken to the fact that there was no place, the way the house was arranged, in which I could have a workroom, not even a bedroom-turned-study, for there was no bedroom to spare. However, the offer was refused, much to our relief.

The house we found is three miles from the one we leave. It is even more accessible to mundane things like railway stations, yet stands a little high above a quiet country road. Built in 1800, it has the look of solidity, of generations, never achieved by the most beautiful modern house in the world. There are three chimneys, which puzzles me—for of fireplaces, only two. The floors are hand-pegged, the color of dark honey. There's an old, high-vaulted barn, a tiny, tumble-down playhouse, and six wild acres which have of late been neglected. From within the house, and the knoll on which it stands, there's a glimpse of the distant Sound. On clear days the Long Island shore floats into view like a mirage. The land back of the house slopes downward, punctuated with ancient apple trees, with willow, dogwood, maple, and pear. At the foot of the slope a brook travels through a triangle of woods, another flows into it, and together they dart underground only to pop up into an irregular, small pool, which a former owner dug out and partly ledged. When the rains come the water is channeled off between and over stones, emptying into a stretch of woods.

Everything native to the house we left is here: the trees, the bushes—there are in fact older, taller trees and a few we never had, including a mammoth mulberry. Storms have cut it down, they tell me, to a third its spread but now from the great trunks the branches rise fan-shaped and the berries attract a multitude of birds. There are also two small mulberries, and once we have rescued them from parasite vines there'll be a white spring parade of dogwoods along a stone wall boundary—a dozen of them.

Lilacs, white and purple, in the spring, carpets of violets, regiments of jack-in-the-pulpits along one brook, a spate of berrybushes, including blueberry. Old roses, sprawling in the sun, too many peony bushes to count, and everywhere lavish iris. Once the property has been cleaned out, it shall remain wild. No more manicured grounds!

Our romantic hearts rejoice in views from an upstairs porch, a bluebird swinging on the green bough, and in the fact that our next-door neighbors are nuns.

Between us and their house there are grass, great trees, plowed fields. We have seen them walking there, and suddenly the landscape is not New England but France. Far beyond where the road turns, twisting up a hill, is a seminary. The bells ring, we can hear them. This is a very peaceful spot. And we did not realize how much we needed peace.

But we are not altogether romantic, we are also practical. Though exposed beams in two rooms upstairs enchant us, we are happy to know the driveway is exceedingly short—which means no snowplow—and that the roofs are of slate.

By the time August comes the move will have been accomplished. All the books that I have chosen will sit on the study shelves—for there is a study—and on those built into the other rooms. The furniture and pictures will look at home, even the rugs and curtains fit. If only we could press buttons and be transported together with our goods and chattels without the customary concomitants of moving, aching feet, painful backs, and dust in the sinuses!

It is obvious to us that there is a good deal to be done, quite apart from the clearing of the grounds and the rescue of a little garden from the ubiquitous jungle of weed and vine. For the time being we must forget that cedars grow up through pines and honeysuckle tangles everywhere. We must think of matters like a new heating system.

First things first, the necessary things, those compatible with comfort. After that, the small amount of remodeling, done slowly, the fitting of a house to a family, like a glove.

Nothing worth while is achieved with ease and dispatch, I think. Between one house and the other lie the innumerable tasks, the packing and discarding, the weariness, the decisions. All through the spring I lay awake pondering upon minute details: the notifications of change of address, the interminable legalities, the wrenching steps one is forced to take. But eventually these are taken; we depart, and arrive.

Curiously enough, the house is in miniature the one we must leave. It's older, and much quieter because of its situation, but the features are there. For a study and a library there're the two in one; for a sunporch downstairs there's a bigger one upstairs; for a big stone terrace there's a small one tucked into a much less public angle of the house, away from the road—a fine place for breakfasting, for a tray lunch, a light supper, as the birds call from the trees and the sun starts to set. For forty-six lilacs—far too many—count six or eight, and instead of four great beds of valley lilies, look for, and find, one—but it will spread.

I have come to the conclusion that life was never intended to mark time or remain static. We had done in fifteen years all that could be done to the home we bought in 1936—planting, planning.

Nothing remained but to, as they say, keep it up. In those three words there is an almost superhuman effort, for in these times assistance is not easily come by and, when it comes at all, bears a high price tag. Now we start over again, and in reclamation, rehabilitation, and the making of a house into home, there is always excitement and interest. This time we must do it cautiously and slowly, bit by bit. This time no new building and very little planting. This time, once the furnace is in, the well and the chimneys checked, no swarm of workmen. I recall a summer in which twenty-two men ran busily over grounds and house, and for months.

That house was for four growing children and two adults. Therefore, six bedrooms and four baths, two upstairs dens, a utility room; therefore, for the assistance we needed and could then procure, a cottage and also, over the garage, an apartment. Now we are two women alone, with one of the children home for weekends, the others for occasional visits. So three bedrooms to start, and two baths, suit us very well, and at a later date the second floor back will yield a bedroom-study for the boy who will be working in New York—if not on the high seas as a Reservist in the U.S. Navy. There'll be a bed on the sleeping porch and one in the attic, in reserve, for the youngsters who may come home.

I have been wondering if there is black alder, the true American holly, on the new property. It likes swamps, and I recall one dark November day when, returning by train from Boston in a driving rain, I saw numbers of them blazing bright and red, a flag of courage along the way. We had some in the old place. What about the new? I can't identify it before the berries come, so I shall wait till autumn to see. If there's none, we'll buy two or three and set them out in the damp ground in the woods, and let them grow there to hearten us when the year turns dark and sullen, when the rain beats down, slants across the windows, and the wind has in it a feel of early snow.

Now, in a measure, we travel light, as befits folk no longer young. We take with us only what we need, augmented by the most treasured things collected over the years. For a time we will keep these cherished, if not necessary, adjuncts to living packed away; little by little we will find or build space for them; eventually they will come out of hiding and become part of the house we live in. But only those inanimate objects which speak to us with too strong a voice to ignore—the ivories my grandfather brought from China at the end of his mission there, the old, lovely things brought also from China by family or friends: a pair of rice bowls and a plate from the imperial factories, a Sung bowl of celadon, a Goddess of Mercy in Ming *blanc de chine*, the loveliest of the snuff-bottle collection and of the little boxes . . .

Space, too, for the Sheraton knife caddy, the tea caddy, and for family photographs, as well as the framed Staffordshire pomade lid, the tiny petit-point landscape I made for my mother when I was miles from home in Germany in 1914, and the farmhouse picture created in wool, embroidered by a member of the family now gone from us.

I believe this is what God intended, a moving on, a winnowing, a starting over again, not on the same scale, not an effort to accumulate, as before, but a return to essentials, keeping only those possessions essential to living, to a reasonable amount of comfort together with those important to heart or spirit. Things that stand for love and friendship, as the old brush holders and scholar's armrest that are on my desk.

The children are now saddled with bits and pieces of family silver, with the pictures that once hung in their rooms, with china and glass. But they are young, the polishing, dusting, washing, will not be as burdensome to them. All these they remember from their growing up, transplanted from their old home to their new homes; they will speak to them of continuity. Come Christmas we will not have as great a tree, so I shall send to the two who will have their own trees the less-fragile ornaments; some date back a quarter of a century. These they can preserve for their children.

It's a curious thing how, once having come to a

decision, once having faced whatever you must know of grief or regret, you find the spirit rallies and goes eagerly forward.

Recently we saw a motion picture called *Beaver Valley*, photographed in color, dealing mainly with the life, times, and hard labor of the beaver. But there were other characters, all manner of beasts and birds. These played themselves against an incomparable background. And a week or so later I read a long article on the ways of the bee. And it seemed incomprehensible to me, as it always does, that there are people who do not believe in God. Surely only the Great Intelligence could create the wonders in the world, the marvelous ingenuity of animals, birds, insects, the wheeling of the stars, the fidelity of sunrise. These are not accidents. But the man who does not believe says carelessly, "Nature."

Of course, nature . . . but certainly that is only the manifestation of God.

Fading summer is a haze upon the hills, dust upon the drooping leaf; already in the high sections, in the mountains not too far away, a leaf here and there is brushed with warning red. It is altogether fitting that when autumn comes blazing, with winter on its heels, we should be settled in the new house, the first hearthfires burning, the old walls closing around us, not as prison walls but as quiet arms. And then we shall look forward, not back, as He who will be with us in this house, as in every other, intended.

3. ❀ *Always Christmas*

I once wrote a short story about a girl, homesick for New England, spending her first Christmas in the tropics. No editor liked it well enough to publish it, but I believe it had a factual and a spiritual truth. For in it her young husband pointed out to her that the birthplace of Jesus was not white with snow nor sharp with cold, that the trees which sang together then were palm trees, not pine nor balsam. And so she came to learn that the Christmas climate lies in the heart and soul.

All summer we have witnessed the slow turning of earth's wheel, in the house, new to us and alive with so many workmen that only before eight-thirty mornings and after four-thirty afternoons could we hear ourselves think. But time has gone so quickly. As you grow older the seasons tread upon one another's heels. Now it's summer, tomorrow autumn, and then you wake to carols and look ahead to spring.

Although we did not see the spring bloom here nor the first returning birds, we had their summer visit—a cloud of birds, a multitude of bunnies performing for us every early evening. And in the autumn come the stranger birds, on the way south, stopping here overnight, or for a day or two, as any traveler stops at (he trusts) a pleasant hotel. So, up go the feeders, and we shall hope for guests who will linger all winter, mindful, however, that we must continue to provide food and drink.

At the other house there had been many feeders, and we brought them along. There each Christmas season we cut a small cedar in the woods and set it between the terrace stones and trimmed it for the birds' Christmas tree. Well wrapped against the chill, we strung popcorn and cranberries like jeweled necklaces, took little pine cones and filled them with peanut butter, hung balls of suet, branches of black alder and bayberry, and somehow managed to tie on quartered apples. It was a pleasing task and we felt that the St. Francis who loved birds gave us his blessing.

This season we need not move a tree. There are two small fat spruces at the front door, and another at one end of the terrace. One of these growing trees shall be for the birds.

Our Christmas decorations, some of which have survived five and twenty years, did not come here in the movers' vans but with us in the family car. From these doors the old felt angels will fly, and the music boxes will sit as always on a desk, on a mantel or table. There will be no difference here. How could there be?

But I am reminded how much smaller the household! It has steadily been shrinking. Fifteen years ago we were six—four children, their godmother, and I. Indeed we were apt to be eight, or ten, what with visiting friends.

People have asked, "Won't this be a strange Christmas with the children gone or, at the very best, only one to come and cry the greeting? Won't it be a little sorrowful too, remembering the past Christmases?" And I can reply with all my heart, and in honesty, that it will be wonderful. It always is. For "wonderful" means full of wonder, and he who has not been full of wonder upon the Eve and Day that we celebrate as Christ's must all his life go bare.

I have never outgrown my childhood excitement, the heart on tiptoe. Oh, the trappings are part of it, the smell of baking, the tree we trim, the decorations we place each year in the same places, the family gifts piling up in the chests, in my study, and hidden in bureau drawers, the gifts from away which I still shake a little as they come in, trying to guess, but not wanting really to know, the cards, the flowers and plants. And part of it the carol singing out of doors with hundreds of neighbors around the lighted, living tree, and the church service after, and coming home to hang the stockings. But this is only a part. The rest of it is the awareness of gentleness and loving-kindness, one for another; the rest of it is the supreme knowledge that we worship at the Manger.

So, no matter how few or how many we shall be, Christmas is always. Nothing is lost to us: not the children who are far away, nor the boy of our blood who sleeps in Arlington; not the parents we knew but now know only in our hearts and spirits. Not even the little dog, much beloved, who spent ten Christmases with us and had her own stocking hung from the mantel and who grew more and more excited as the packages came in. For she lies dreaming under a tree three miles away, where once she lived. She was never happy here, ill, in a strange place and her young idol no longer here, so when she died, we took her back to a familiar place. She isn't lost to us, and she belongs in this Christmas story. Just as I often dream of my father, or look at the faded pictures of my grandparents, or of my Quaker people, or think of my mother as she was, I think of the cocker spaniel who shared our Christmases, and hear her paws upon the stairs.

Surely it can *always* be Christmas! If only we had the pity and the patience, the love and the wisdom. If only we could carry over from season to season the sense of expectancy, the loving-kindness, the close feeling for those we love, the neighborly feeling for friend and stranger. Look how, at this season, we walk down the street and cry "Merry Christmas" to those we know and those we barely know. We mean it with all our hearts. But it lasts so short a time.

Christmas is here, then over. In our locality there is the winter quiet, the cold and wind, the storm, the branches breaking, the possible blizzard, disaster or inconvenience. And soon, winter-weary, we long for spring, the first bird voice, the breaking blossom, the blue sky, the warmth . . . we are impatient, we have short memories and Christmas lies behind us.

Or so we think.

It lies always ahead: it lies always in the heart. Look at the spring through the eyes of Christmas; Christmas is a Birth, and spring a Rebirth. Christmas is promise and fulfillment, and spring again the promise and fulfillment. All the year is linked with Christmas—it runs through the twelve months like a golden thread, it binds them together.

For to the believing heart, the spirit upon its knees, there is no day nor season without Christ, the Newborn and the Risen.

Christmas is always.

AUGUST

1. ❀ *Lift Up Your Eyes*

I have written a good deal about prayer. I have described how it springs, spontaneously, from the troubled or grateful heart and mind. I know the miracle of prayer from personal experience and so I write from deep down. I fervently believe what I say.

Some readers write me that they have experienced the same things, if in different ways. It was with enormous pleasure that one day last spring a stranger, having recognized me, spoke to me in a pleasant roadside restaurant. It seemed that two months previously she had sold her house and was looking for a new one. Somehow she had found my little piece, among her mother's treasured copies of the *Christian Herald*, on how we sold ours. She took it to her husband to read because, she said, "We're in the same boat."

Today I want to write again about prayer—about the times that afflict many of us when suddenly prayer seems impossible. This, too, has happened to me. It is as if the fallow ground, for years nourished and enriched by rain and sun, becomes, in an instant, hopelessly sterile.

This sometimes happens, not because we lose our faith in prayer or have prayed for something and not received it, nor even because we have suffered a great loss which we cannot comprehend. It comes, I believe, because of some inner conflict during which we reach a point, one known only to ourselves, when we dare not and cannot look for release or comfort or guidance.

It is not difficult to pray, indeed, it is the easiest thing in the world, to pray for another's safety, welfare, consolation, or happiness. All of us, who believe ourselves to be Christian, do just that every day of our lives. It is also easy to pray for ourselves—that we may be guided, prosper, and find happiness.

But sometimes each of us reaches an impasse where we find that praying for ourselves would, as far as our finite eye can see, injure someone else. In short, if what we wish means our happiness, it could mean someone else's misery. This sets up a conflict which is, I believe, second to almost none. For each of us, the personal happiness or the misery varies, but the conflict is the same.

To take an ordinary example: here is a young person whose parents have sacrificed everything so that he might enter a certain profession. Their hearts are set upon it, but suddenly the son finds that he does not want this, that his true feeling runs in quite another direction. In order to preserve his spiritual independence and what he believes is his personal happiness, he must go to them and say, "I cannot do what you want me to do."

Such a problem creates a tremendous block. The block is guilt. Each is torn, pulled first one way and then the other. Perhaps they believe with all their hearts that they should make another great sacrifice and give up their wishes. Yet they cannot do so. Perhaps they feel, as a dear and brilliant friend of mine wrote me recently, "Sacrifice is only for the saints."

The dilemma in which you often find yourself is a similar one. You try to pray for guidance, yet in a way you don't really want it. If the guidance comes and throws a light upon the path, if you are innerly told you must make the sacrifice, you think, evade, and plead.

Yet you do not dare pray for yourself—for your own wish and happiness. A guilt-block stands in your way. You feel that you are right but at the same time you feel so terribly selfish. Nor can you easily pray for the person who would be injured at your hands. How can you pray for him, or her? What prayer is there? You might pray, of course, for his happiness. Naturally, that is what you should do. But it would be at the expense of your own.

The horns of this dilemma are very sharp, indeed. They pierce both ways. I believe that in such a time you cannot force a prayer of words. You cannot say, "God grant me this," or "Lord let the cup pass," or "Father, spare me." And you are far too human and vulnerable, I suppose, to beseech God to show you the sacrificial path. I believe there is nothing you can do but silently place your problem in God's hands, and wait, neither pleading nor asking nor even forming words in your mind beyond "Father, thy will be done."

This is the sterile time. When such things confront us, no one human being can help. Not family nor even the most trusted clergyman or friend.

I believe that one of the great tragedies in all our lives is that we so often bring sorrow, disillusionment, or even great harm to people who in no way deserve it. They are the guiltless, the completely innocent. Sometimes we do it unwittingly, sometimes circumstances play a part, and sometimes it almost seems as if we cannot help it.

But we cannot see ahead. We cannot know. We grope in the darkness and beat against rock with bare hands and tear ourselves to shreds, and find ourselves not an inch further along.

Then it is that we must reach the point where we cannot, and dare not, retire into the quiet room of the spirit and pray for ourselves nor for anyone else. This is the last extremity, and we can only try to relax the inner tensions and to place the burden before God.

Driving about the summer countryside, I see the trees in full leaf, the summer gardens replenished by those who tend them, the little streams bounding zestfully along, the bright blue sky and hills beyond, the fat and lazy clouds. Certainly, the hills beyond, rounding and rolling, give one in trouble a sense of reassurance. It is one of the unfortunate blows struck at the troubled that real disaster, realized or impending, takes from him all interest in man-made things and people.

The Psalmist knew about this reassurance when he said, "I will lift up mine eyes unto the hills, from whence cometh my help."

The hills around us are of soil and stone. They were created by God through the slow centuries, through glacial beginning, floods, erosion. A thousand things have gone into their making. They are natural, being of Nature. They are also enduring. They have the strength that undergoes no change.

Lifting up your eyes is probably as important as

anything you can do. When you are beset upon all sides by a trouble, usually of your own making, your eyes are cast down. They see only the ground upon which you walk, inch by inch; the present crossroads, the path you feel you must choose. They see only a very little because the eyes are human. They do not take the long view. But to make the effort to lift the sight from the ground to the far hills is also to lift the heart and the spirit. It is then you most fully realize that you do not travel alone.

The hills look down, yet are not indifferent. I do not for a moment believe that what happens to each of us, however unimportant it may seem, is really unimportant. I believe everything is vital to us, to our growth, to our lives and to the lives of those we influence or love. I believe that everything about us is important to God. As it is said, the fall of a sparrow also is marked. I think the natural hills and those which can be seen only by the raised eyes of the spirit are there to tell us that they are the help and strength and patience that accompany and console us.

I have found—and I am certain that many of you reading this have also found—that the effort is worth it. Once you have lifted your eyes to what lies above you find strength, for surely God is mindful of His child's trouble. If it is brought to Him in humility and left with Him, it must be resolved.

It is not always resolved as we might wish. But I do believe there is a way. When in weakness and perplexity we cannot find this way ourselves we are led to it through prayer. Once it has been found, the sterile days are over, and the prayers well up as naturally as springs flow or grass grows.

Even when life's problems grow too heavy to endure, we must turn to God in prayer. But, I believe, a prayer of words is not necessary. Whether we cannot or whether we dare not pray with words is not important. The important thing is that He knows this and has compassion.

However guilty or self-obsessed, however unworthy our lives, these are ours—God's compassion and mercy and His hills from which strength comes.

2. *Four Seasons, Three Tenses*

Time is a dressmaker specializing in alterations. In August, in this climate, the days are hot and humid but the nights begin to freshen. I am a four-seasons person. I would not like living in a climate in which the seasons were not sharply defined, for instance, in the tropics, where winter is represented mostly by the continuous, heavy rains. In New England, Nature entertains herself now and then by producing balmy winter days or a perishing cold spell in spring or early summer. Often there's a stretch of autumn weather which simulates spring, and there were days last May when, waking to wind and crisp chill, we were sure it was fall! But, by and large, we are furnished with four seasons, and of these I believe I care least for summer.

Perhaps this has something to do with age. I certainly remember, as a child, looking forward to summer with the greatest anticipation, for then summer's coming meant the end of school and ahead the long vacation; it meant visiting and being visited, swimming, boating, fishing, parties and picnics.

In summer, nowadays, the trees seem to grow listless and dusty, the highways are so crowded that we seldom attempt even a short trip. We battle daily with the voracious insect and mutter about humidity. And it becomes an effort to do a day's work at a desk.

However, there are pleasures—iced tea on a terrace, a supper tray. The long and golden evenings, the wildflower, the rose and lily and the very early morning—all these have a certain enchantment. But I am still prejudiced in favor of autumn and spring with, believe it or not, a leaning toward winter, which once I despised. I am still terrified of icy roads, sleet, and driving to the village under adverse conditions. But I have grown to enjoy a bad day, even with thick snow and zero temperatures, if I am indoors. It is satisfying to sit by a window, nursing a cup of tea, hearing the fire snap on the hearth, and watching the wild-white world outside, kept at bay by good walls and insulation. I like the stark shapes of trees. It's as if their true character emerged, stripped of trimmings. Also, the winter weather is conducive to hard work; I don't want to go anywhere, and seldom can. The cupboard is stocked, and the freezer. So, I stay home and work!

There was a time when I took seasons for granted. Yet, as one grows older, it is evident that nothing should be taken for granted—not even the simple everyday phrases we all use. It was not until recently that I stopped to remember what "goodbye" means. I suppose we all say the word twenty times a day. How often do we recall that it means "God be with you"? And when we sign our letters "sincerely" or "truly" or "cordially," how much do we mean it?

All of us experience the lean and the fat years. And with the incurable optimism of most human hearts we are certain that bad times cannot long endure. But we are equally sure that the good times will last indefinitely, which is not too practical a view. However, if one is old enough to look back over a decade or two, or three, one will see clearly that in most lives the good and bad achieve a balance. I remember a period of some ten months during which I underwent several quite unrelated operations. I was appalled, unresigned; I felt singled out for disaster. But afterward I thought back and remembered the many years during which I had escaped illness of any sort. I'd had the peculiar theory that everyone else was susceptible to serious illness except myself.

Looking back, I realized I'd taken my "invulnerability" for granted. Now, having learned the hard way, I know better.

When I was a girl and living the long summer through on my father's place on Shelter Island, I used to be entertained by his custom of sitting on the big porch and spying upon the birds through binoculars. He was a trial lawyer, and in those days the courts closed for much of the summer. He had a wonderful time watching the orioles build their intricate nests. At times I thought him slightly daft, especially when I would come up from our beach through the apple orchard with a group of lively friends, and there Father would be making wild gestures. We were to be silent, go on tiptoe, avoiding the old pear tree sacred to the oriole and taking care not to interrupt their home building.

At that time my interest in birds was nil. They had feathers and they flew. They built nests, laid eggs and hatched them; they sang sweetly. But I do not think that I acquired any real affection for birds until we moved to the country. That was when I began to buy bird books and to leap from my desk and dash into the garden in order to track down a strange bright visitor or a new song.

In our house, bird watching is simple, since all the many windows look out upon vistas—the little hill, the birdbath, the feeders, the trees. The birds are as curious as we. They like to take a look at how the other half lives, or perhaps identify the species, for they sit up on the crowding branches and blandly look in at bedroom or sunporch windows.

In the living room, the picture window facing east looks down a slope to the pond, and the maple and apple trees, the dogwood and shagbark hickory stand sentinel. There's a big chair at that window; beside it is a small table. And on the table, a pair of binoculars. A great many times a day I sit down, take up the glasses, and look down the slope to the pond. Very often I see mallards, one or two pairs, walking around it or swimming on the surface. I see the pheasant come from the brush to feed at the pan of corn we keep near the pond's edge. Or, I look into the far trees at a brilliant bird flying or a hawk perching atop a limb of a dead tree. It never occurred to me until a few weeks ago how like my father I have become! And then I came upon the realization with regret, for how much I might have contributed to his pleasure had I shared his interest!

This is one of the saddest things about growing up, and I mean *really* growing up. It is impossible not to look back over your shoulder and remember the sins of omission, the word unsaid, the assurance of gratitude or affection unspoken. I believe most of us feel this way. And nothing can be done about it, of course. It is scant consolation to think that our children and grandchildren may one day feel about us as we do now about those of our family who have gone away. But I hold fast to a belief that those we loved and still love, those who loved and still love us, are somehow given an insight into our hearts.

The child lives in the present. The past is unknown to him, the future too difficult for him to grasp. From one wonderful Christmas to the next, from one happy summer to another, is a period which seems too long to contemplate. The young adult lives in the present and the foreseeable future, but older people grow into a sort of three-dimensional viewpoint. The past, the present, and the future merge and become in a sense one, compounded of happiness and grief, satisfaction and regret. The past, too, soon becomes the present and the future, not nearly so far off as once we imagined, seems to shrink.

I do not consider it healthy to live in the past. Folks do, of course, becoming nostalgic, refusing to believe that any time is as good as that which has run out. These are the people who are unable to enjoy the beauty and wonder of today or anticipate the greater beauty and wonder of tomorrow. They forget all that was unhappy about the past, think little of the future, and so live in a narrowing world. We say of them that they do not move with the times. It might be more truly said they are not moved by the events of the present.

It is sounder, I dare say, to take only from the past that is peculiarly your own—and merely the past that is historical and common to all who are your contemporaries—and extract from it the distillation of your young happiness and growth. As for the future, we must learn that we are not to be afraid. The present is still our own.

I have for some time felt that to walk daily, with the knowledge that the earthly future no longer stretches, indefinitely, before me can only lengthen the great joy in living, which is one of God's most wonderful gifts to His children. It is trite to say that as you grow older you find, if you are fortunate, infinite pleasure in simple things. However trite, it is solid truth, as most "trite" things are basically true. Take, for example, the free-flying birds which, in the period of my youth, meant so little and now mean so much. And when spring comes I am excited by the first faint sheen of the trees, the first courageous flower in the woods, the first bursting into bloom of the common shrub—all manifestations which for so many years I largely ignored, except to note in passing that winter had gone and spring was on the way. But now I am grateful to have been granted still another spring, another summer, another autumn, when the torch is set to our section of the country and life goes to its temporary sleep in a bonfire of beauty. Grateful, too, for still another winter, white and wonderful, never the end of growth, merely the rest period, a recess, and always the signpost pointing the way to awakening.

Not long ago a very dear friend asked me if I ever awoke mornings "feeling suicidal." She did not, of course, mean it literally. But I answered, and truly, as if she had so meant it. I said, "No." I said that no matter how despairing I had been before I slept, oppressed by this or the other problem, I always woke happy that I *did* wake, for waking meant another day, another opportunity, another chance to find a solution to whatever puzzle had sent me to bed anxious and disturbed. And it meant also an awareness, a chance to enjoy the good that the day would surely bring, whether work or friends, the long-awaited letter, the possibility of good news, a hope which is never extinguished, one or more of the simple pleasures each of us can freely enjoy.

During my lifetime I have gone to bed many times to say desperate prayers in the dark, to be awake grieving or wondering or fearing. The events that brought about the state of fearful mind and downcast spirit are those which, sooner or later, reach us all in some degree. They include the common sorrows and problems that all who are mortal must experience, each in his own fashion, whether the death of someone dear or an illness which could terminate a beloved life, or the material anxieties or changes that must alter everything. There are hundreds of anxieties and sorrows which send the spirit to its knees: work, its difficulty or absence, the mistake made yesterday, which you feel you can never rectify, the disloyalty to another, which you regret, or another's disloyalty to you, which is as a thorn in your heart. All these I have known, yet I cannot recall a time when, the night past, however anguished or fearful, I was not glad to awaken to a new day.

The new day cannot assuage the grief caused by irreparable loss, but it can, and does, bring the courage to face it. It brings the determination to find the problem's solution, and the renewed belief that your child, or your friend, or your predicament is in God's hands.

As children and young people, we wake and take the new day for granted. But I think we must awaken with gratitude when many of our days lie behind us. For waking means life, and it is slowly borne in upon us that the future is not, after all, a short one as the sun declines. For where there is winter there is also spring, where there is night the morning follows. And God, who gave us life upon the beautiful earth, has done much more. He has given us life everlasting.

SEPTEMBER

1. ❀ *The Way*

No matter what summer or autumn brings, there will be folks who will complain. They will bewail April if it is rainy, they will protest the cold winds of winter, crying out that spring never comes. Or, if May arrives with a blast of heat, they will say, "But we've had no spring, we've been shoved right into summer." Or May may arrive with chilling mornings. Then cotton dresses will be grumblingly returned to the clothes closet in exchange for the woolens which have just been laid in moth balls. Or perhaps the weather will be exactly what these folks say they want it to be. No matter—they wail, they complain. If the weather is good, they will say it is too good to last. If it is bad, they will sulk as if it would never be good again.

Despite the puzzling antics of human beings—and our depressing news headlines, which nowadays seldom herald a happy event—I still have an unbounded faith in people. Recently I spoke extemporaneously at a church meeting. I don't know what it did to my audience but, as so often happens with other people who have occasion to speak, what I said later set me to pondering. You know how it is—you get up on your feet and say something quite "off the top of your head," and then later you find yourself wondering about it. It's often that way with writing. I have on occasion begun to outline for an editor merely the basic idea of a story that has just come to me and before I know it I am pouring out five times as much story material as I thought I had.

In my talk at the church I brought out the fact that during my life I had seen more good than evil, more kindness than cruelty, more generosity than meanness, more love than hate. Perhaps I have forgotten many things that once hurt and rankled. Even so, I still believe that there is a basic fairness and order and balance in the world. Sincerely seek what you want, and you will find it. Give of yourself, and it will be returned in kind. Look for the good qualities in a person, and there they will be. Or suddenly decide that the same person is but a mass of faults and shortcomings—and, incredibly enough, *that* is what you will find him to be. This is no Pollyanna notion someone just dreamed up. It is a fundamental and immutable law of life.

Whenever I speak of the goodness of life, someone is always bound to say, "But you forget wars and disease and poverty." I've lived long enough to remember several wars. And I've seen poverty and disease. But war, poverty, and disease are all parts of an immutable law. Almost invariably man-made, they spring from greed, ignorance, or fear. Science strives —and often succeeds in banishing this or that disease. Yet when one disease has been eradicated, another often arises. Whenever I say this, people ask, "Would you place such calamities as earthquakes and floods in the same category?" My answer is that no one can tell if this little earth we know is not still in the process of being completed. The mountains move and the great waters shift and the guilty and innocent alike are hurt.

Yet I am not unduly perturbed by our modern prophets of doom who wail at us from newspapers, books, and lecture platforms about the pitfalls that lie ahead. I don't know much about history—but this I do know: since the dawn of time men have lived through war and disease and catastrophe. And we of this era are faced with no trials and tribulations—including our "alarming" juvenile delinquency—

that haven't been problems on this earth for a very, very long time.

Our little world has survived much. It will go on surviving. There is a sort of steel which reinforces people in times of major disaster. And from these disasters often come good things—for they are "the other side of the coin." Take, for example, the enormous outpouring of concern and generous aid when some part of our country is stricken with catastrophe. (And it doesn't always have to be our country.) Even war has been known to produce good things—such as miraculous new life-giving drugs. Or it produces people who set inspiring examples of courage, moral endurance, and sacrifice for others. Or war may give rise to people who are more determined than ever to banish war for all time. Whatever it may be—war, disease, or disaster—such events draw people closer together in a bond of brotherhood rarely achieved in times of tranquillity.

When speaking before some groups I sometimes astonish or even affront them by saying that I do not believe that we have a sectarian God, who expresses Himself only through this or that church. Nor do I believe that the great Divine Intelligence—which planned the universe and set the stars and seasons and human cycles into motion—is much concerned with the type of edifice in which we worship, or what we say there, or even how we address ourselves to Him. I believe He is concerned with the spirit within us, which is a part of His own consciousness. God did not make you or me exclusively. He made all mankind—and all in His image.

A small boy may understand little of the prayers he learns to repeat after his mother. Yet when he runs out on a sunlit hillside and sees an autumn leaf which has begun to flame, or the first blossom of summer, or a lone bird winging from the earth, or a single snowflake lazing to earth—he may learn at first hand much about God. Without worry or ceremony, he is simply a part of the great living universe around him. And thus he will be part of the Creator. I have always felt that this was what Jesus was trying to make us understand when He said, "Of such is the kingdom of heaven."

Sometimes when things get difficult, and one problem piles on top of the other, I find myself reaching a point where I can no longer act or even think. At such times I do what I've just had my hypothetical little boy do. I take a moment to look at the world around me. It may be only from a window from which I can see but a few trees and bushes, or perhaps a spot of water, or just a small slice of sky. No matter. What I see at that moment is the whole universe in miniature—*and I am a part of it.* And with this in mind I sit down and simply let all my cares, worries and tensions drain out of me. And then I say in my mind—or perhaps out loud—what with me is an old prayer. I do not ask for any one specific thing, but merely for just enough help so that I can help myself. And after a while—with that precious moment spent patiently and serenely in trying to reach the great Source—I get up and walk away, and find that I am thinking and acting just as well as before. For if ever there was a great truth uttered—and it has been repeated again and again down through the centuries—it is: "You are never alone." It takes quite a while to learn this. Some of us never wholly learn it. Some learn it only through desolation and grief. And some fortunate ones are born knowing it.

2. *Time, You, and I*

Lately I've been thinking a great deal about Time. It's something everyone thinks about occasionally. And so I suppose it is a bromide to remind people how one's sense of time alters with the years. The time pattern we live by—a calendar counting the days and months, a clock ticking off the seconds and minutes—is actually quite artificial. What is considerably more real is time as we live it inside ourselves.

Remember, when we were children, what an eternity stretched from one birthday to the next, from one Christmas to another? And how interminable was the school term, how brief the holiday? Yet as we grew older time began to shrink. So that by the time we reached middle age it seemed that the Christmas decorations were scarcely put away before they had to be brought out again. There never seemed time enough to do what we wanted. The beds would hardly be made and the breakfast dishes washed before it was time to start dinner. Time was forever nipping at our heels.

Yet, take the last war. No matter how fast it rushed past for some people, it dragged endlessly for the families of men in training camps and overseas. For them time was heartbreakingly long between letters and home-coming furloughs.

There is nothing fixed about time. It's entirely flexible and relative. When your babies are small you actually wonder if they will ever grow up, and if the day will ever come when they will be self-reliant. Then with shocking suddenness they are grown—and sorrowfully you think, "They grow up too fast. One minute they are in the cradle, the next they are graduating from high school." Life, I believe, has always been like that. Always it is lived at two speeds: one in which the days zip past with jet-propelled swiftness, the other at which the days drag by with leaden feet.

It is a true saying that we begin to die as soon as we are born. Some of us wish a day would never end. Yet others, having lived the day as fully as possible, are glad when night finally falls. It's an odd thing about time. You can't stop it, start it, speed it up, or slow it down—except by the manner in which you live it.

I believe that for God, and for those who look life honestly in the face, there is really no such thing as time, space, future, past or even present—for all are encompassed in one. And so I think that in considering life only the longest view should be taken, rather than the very short one of the body's brief life span on earth. I believe in the continuance of the spirit, which is the essence of the personality. And I believe in the endurance through all time—however it is measured—of the wonder and essence of human love.

If a man's spirit is not immortal, then it is nothing. For there is little point in having lived, suffered, painfully learned, and slowly progressed if it is all to be wasted. No—Christ has proved to us that the spirit lives forever. There is no waste.

Love, too, is immortal. In the love of men and women, of parents for their children, of man for his fellow man whether he be friend or stranger—here, too, is deathlessness of the spirit. Because someone close to us leaves us for a short while, a long while, or even forever, must we cease to love him?

We all know people who believe themselves to be unusually cherished—magnetic, charming, entertaining people whom everyone wants to have around. It must be a dreadful shock to these people later to discover, as very often they do, that they were not nearly so cherished as they had once believed. And that they were wanted only because they were charming, amusing, openhanded. These are delightful qualities, to be sure, but they are not likely to be long remembered. On the other hand, many a shy, quiet, obscure man who had always considered himself dull and routine has discovered, after a long absence, that he was deeply cherished and profoundly missed. Charm is undeniably charming, while integrity is seldom spectacular; and sheer goodness often appears dull on the surface. Yet in the long run it is the truly good man who is the remembered man.

The true love that man bears for friends and strangers alike, be they close or distant, is a never-ending circle. It does not cease, because it cannot cease. Such love is the reflection of God's love for humanity. It is the reflection of the love for which Christ sacrificed Himself in order to bring us redemption, resurrection, and the knowledge that the spirit lives forever.

Nothing in this world is as true as the fact that we are part of God, that He is within us and we are in Him. It is our reflection of the Divine Spirit, the unfailing Intelligence, the enduring Love—which makes us thinking and feeling people. It lifts us far above the animal state. At times it even carries us a shade above our own bodily mortality. All of us have known ordinary people who have overcome problems and surmounted difficulties by what were almost superhuman achievements. Yet it has been but a reaching out and up, a drawing upon a great inner

Power, which has enabled these fallible hum beings to rise to unbelievable heights.

How often have we heard someone say of a des perately trying period, "I don't know how I lived through it." Well, I know, and so do you. The trying period was endured and conquered by an inner strength which exists in all of us, and which is there for us to draw on whenever we need it. The great pity is that we use it as little as we do, for it is a strength which is increased rather than diminished with use.

Our beginnings are in yesterday, we think, but they are also in today and tomorrow. In fact, I sometimes wonder if there really *are* three tenses. All the time there is, or was, or ever will be is all around us at this very moment. If we accept this interpretation of time, then nothing is lost.

Time is important only in the use we make of it—in living it to the fullest, which includes the contemplative life of the spirit, the growing in wisdom and stature, and the awareness that this growth, unlike that of mind and body, will never end. And Love, too, is important—but only in so far as we use it in warmth, companionship, and understanding, and in that deeper use in which the exchange of love brings mutual nourishment.

OCTOBER

I. ꕥ *October 3*

During World War II, five boys of my blood went, and returned: three, my sister's sons; two, mine. At the time of their enlistments their ages ranged from seventeen to twenty. Their services were in the infantry, the Navy, and the Marines. Two were wounded, two did not experience actual combat. And for us at home the long years of anxiety finally ended; we believed, for good.

But the youngest, my sister's son, younger by three weeks than the younger boy in our house, remained in the Army, selecting it as his profession. At twenty he was a first lieutenant, and before he was twenty-one, a married man.

In July, 1950, shortly before he expected to sail

for Germany, he was sent from Fort Lewis, with the 8th Infantry, in the 2nd Division, to Korea. This time he left not only parents, brothers, and a sister but his young wife, a little son, and an unborn child.

On September 23 his wife was safely delivered of a baby girl, on the 24th she learned that her husband was missing, and on October 2 that he was dead . . . killed in action.

This intelligence reached me upon the evening of the same day. I was completely stunned and confused for a time, and then I forced myself to believe it, but rebellious, unresigned, and blind with a strange, dark anger impossible to describe. I kept thinking: the old men make these wars, the young men die in the horror and devastation, the mud and agony.

Personal grief is one thing; you suffer it alone, it is yours. But grief for others is something else again. If someone close to us undergoes pain of flesh or spirit—or someone we barely know, or even, it may be, a stranger—we all experience, in varying degrees, what is termed sympathy. But there is also something called empathy . . . and it is different. If, for instance, you see someone in pain you are sorry, you sympathize. But if you actually *feel* that pain in your own flesh—or spirit, as the case may be—that is empathy.

October 3, like the preceding day, was very beautiful in our part of New England. Blue and windless, warm and golden. The four walls of the house closed in on me. Together with a member of my family I got into a car and we drove without planned direction, upstate. I could not be with my sister; she was in Texas, with her daughter-in-law and grandchildren.

The sun was like a blessing and the leaves were beginning to turn their wonderful shifting colors. It was lunchtime when we reached the quiet town of Woodbury. We had no desire to find a restaurant, a wayside diner, or a drugstore. One of us suggested a picnic.

So, we stopped at a grocery store and bought milk and cookies, and other things, paper cups, plates, some sliced meat, a little cake, and then drove out on Route 67 on which we knew there was a small state-owned picnic place.

There were not many people there on that quiet Tuesday: a boy and girl sitting at a table, talking; a group of elderly women, walking along the riverbank, and then driving off again; a married couple washing the car.

We took our lunch to the battered bench at a table, and sat down, and ate a little. The other people were not close by, we could not even hear their voices. No wind spoke in the trees, but now and then a leaf drifted, soundless, to the earth. The little river was shallow and filled with stones; there was still water there, white over the rocks, and speaking softly as it ran toward its destination. The sun beat down, a wasp invaded our privacy, a bird spoke nearby, a flock of sparrows gathered in conference across the river and then rose in flight.

The little place was known and dear to us. It is a favorite picnic spot of a close friend who lives in Southbury. And once we brought an English friend here, on her first picnic since before the war.

In the feel of the air, warm and silken, in the vagrant breeze that came from nowhere and went back there again, in the clear, quick speech of the river and the reflected color of the leaves, in the trees and quiet, all pervaded by sunlight, there was a great compassionate healing.

We could not remain long, but in the brief space of time the logic of the ultimate survival reached me, as if the little world I saw were a book in which I might read and be convinced. The world itself is a cruel and desperate thing; that is to say, the world that men make with their hands, and brains, their greed and ambition. But the world composed of earth and water, sky and cloud, and all the growing things, this is endearing beauty. Sitting there, thinking of this altering but everlasting pattern, it was impossible for me to believe that my sister's son had not opened his eyes to a world more beautiful and, as he now is, forever young.

In the smaller world of nature there is a continuing pattern. The green leaves of summer blaze out in a glory which is never final. The snow falls, the leaves are gone, the trees stretch dark, bare arms in the sullen sky, and it is winter. But never death. For presently the sleepers awaken and new leaves reach out in tender green, the snow is gone, the birds return, the flowers blossom, and it is spring.

This is, I believe, the great promise, the fulfilled pledge, the symbol, the assurance of immortality. On earth the pattern is broken yet continues. Past earth, there are no seasons; none are needed, for there the pattern is made plain, and is fulfilled.

Once long ago I heard a legend about the ancient weavers of Oriental rugs. How true it is, I do not know. It was said that the pattern was never quite finished, that there was always, as it were, a flaw in it, as the makers believed that, if it were perfect, they must die. Perhaps mortal death is the break in the mortal pattern, and only afterward is the plan made clear, and perfected.

I thought of my nephew. In his brief life he had known great happiness. He was brilliant and mature far beyond his years. He enjoyed a close family life, an education which brought him honors. He was gay, amused and amusing, he had many friends wherever he went. He liked the career he had selected; he was not groping and dissatisfied.

Also, unlike many, he had experienced before his death the joy and responsibility of a happy marriage and of fatherhood, and of deep religious conviction.

At twenty-three, dying, he had lived a fuller life than many men twice his age. And the continuing pattern goes on—in the little son who is too young to remember him, in the daughter who never knew him but whom he also loved.

These are the things of which I thought. I cannot say with any truth that I am resigned even now. I know that to his wife and parents adjustment to grief and emptiness and loss must have come very slowly. I know that words were of no consolation. Consolation lies only—and after a long while—in remembered happiness and in the rooted conviction of the spirit's survival—the last, the ultimate triumph and victory.

Bitterness there must be, rebellion, and the wild unseeing sorrow. Many of us have known these sword thrusts, many more will know them. Each of us, at one time or another, pays a price for whatever joy we treasure, for joy and grief are inescapable in this mortality. The price is almost always unendurably high, we think. Yet we pay it and endure.

For as long as men have gone to war there have been brave words spoken of those who fall in combat—words which deal with sacrifice, with courage, with belief in freedom, with the passion for peace. To many people such words will be of comfort; but beyond all words there is the silence of the spirit, and into such silence comes a great consolation: the belief in the continuing pattern, the belief in God's infinite compassion, and in the promise made to us by His Son . . . who rose from the dead that we might have everlasting life.

2. ꕥ *Important Four-Letter Words*

October is a mattering month to me. On the first of this month I was born, and on the second I learned of my nephew's death. Now he lies in Arlington, having come the long way from Korea. There was an award for him—a Silver Star. But you and I know that there has been another, infinitely greater award and that wherever his bright young spirit shines there are many stars, gold and silver, glowing within the reach of his ageless hand.

With autumn here and winter coming on chilly feet, there will be time to read, long evenings. I can sit down once more and read some of the old books as well as the new. But the new books, in many instances, distress me. I read some over last spring and summer. Many are as steady on the best-seller lists as canned goods on grocery shelves.

I cannot say that I have been shocked, neither by those novels which treat of war or of peacetime armies, nor by those which deal in highly spiced "history," nor yet by the so-called sophisticated fiction, modern as next week. I am not easily shocked by what are, after all, words. I am shocked in the true sense only by tragedy, and cruelty and waste. But by books which rely upon bad language and worse situations for their reader-pull I am saddened and affronted.

Mind you, I have no quarrel with realism. Calling a spade a spade, in an era which turns itself inside out to be "frank," is hardly horrifying. But they don't just call it a spade!

I am not a reactionary, unless to have notions about good taste, decency, and fastidiousness is reactionary. Many very great books, for instance, deal honestly and openly with what we call sex. The Bible for one—the Old Testament. And sex is an elastic little three-letter word which stretches to encompass many meanings: it can be vital, tender; it can be brutal, fatal.

Over the years, since the twenties, writers have gone further and further, leaping over or destroying certain boundaries. Perhaps they will now become frustrated, since there seem to be no more boundaries to leap over or destroy. Twenty years ago, thirty, a writer indicated a curse by a blank—if you wished you filled it in. Later this trick expanded to include the taboo words. Then, in Mr. Hemingway's manner, the word "obscenity" was used instead of the blank to indicate an obscenity. It made for extremely monotonous reading. At least, for me. And I admire Mr. Hemingway except for his deplorable repetition.

Nowadays, however, the newer writers don't bother to let anything represent obscenity. They simply take their typewriters, as it were, and reverting to childhood, they once more write upon the fences and sidewalks.

This is what affronts and saddens, and also bores, me.

I dare say that the majority of adult people now living—and those now dead, for the Restoration period knew a lot of vivid words and used them and the Victorians were a vulgar lot beneath their "refinement"—I dare say they know all the words, or most of them, but most of us never expected to see the fence words or those overheard from the gutter neatly bound, at four dollars a copy, lying on the living-room table.

Take the soldier books, for instance. Any realistic person knows and admits that soldiers in the field, in the barracks, do not speak in poetry. Yet not *all* of them dredge up their limited vocabularies from the gutter. One good war book has been written which avoids the worst of the language. I haven't read it yet. I understand that the author referred to such language as "good-humored Billingsgate" and added something to the effect that it wasn't necessary to report it. Once you have granted that the language of the barracks is not that of everyday conversation, it seems to me unnecessary to be hit in the face with it, as if with a long-dead fish. The story will not suffer, nor will the reader.

One criticism of a widely read best seller was that factual blow-by-blow reporting didn't make for literature. Nor does it. There is nothing of a writer's vision, empathy, or imagination in this; there is merely a keen ear for ugliness. Bad language doesn't really make a character unique or even definite. As a matter of fact, those books, whether or not they contain offensive language, which strive to reproduce exactly the ordinary conversation of ordinary people are not always successful or even interesting.

What bothers me is that people who read "everything" and talk with glibness about the recurrent, so-called four-letter words have completely forgotten, if ever they knew, that there are a great many four-letter words of a different kind. These appear in books and newspapers, old and new, they are heard in the market place, in the churches, on the street, in your own dining room, in the parlor—and few people give them a second thought.

Yet these, and not the others, are the important four-letter words. Let's think about some of them.

There is a word which spells *just.* It has four letters and many writers use it; perhaps not in that way, but that's what they mean. Yet there is also a four-letter word which spells *love.* Writers use that, too—we all do. It is a vital word. You can spell it with a small "l" or a capital. Love comes in many guises and springs from the same Source—love of God, God's love for us. Then there is the human love of family, home, friends, work, the love of country. Given enough of this four-letter word, properly interpreted and put to work, there would be no wars, and no crime and no cruelty.

Love is a four-letter word. None can deny it. And *soul*, which is the very heart of love, has four letters also (but spirit and heart have more) . *Evil* is a four-letter word, and many four-letter words *are* evil, but *good* has four letters also, and I would back those four against the other side of the coin. For good does triumph over evil. This has been promised us, and it is true.

True has four letters, too. And the bright word *glad*. A *star* has five points and four letters, and *wake* and *rise*, and *sing*.

From these four-letter words a man can make a poem, a man can build a life, a man can achieve a goal. All four-letter words.

And, now that I think of it, *life* has four letters . . . four letters which say everything. There is not enough time in a lifetime to say all there is to say about life—little as we really know it—for it encompasses also those opposing words which are "good" and "evil."

Then there is a four-letter word which means comfort and help and wonder, which means praise and fulfillment and strength: that word is *pray*.

Surely these are the important words, the words that matter, the words that are never empty. And is not an essential word just that—Word, *the* Word?

And surely the most important word of all has four letters in French and German, but only three in English, and that is the Word we live by, the Word that is all consolation and all courage, the Word that speaks to the heart and the soul, the greatest Word, however spelled in any language—and in ours, the three letters that spell out *God.*

3. ❀ *Torch Song*

Now that it is again October, my birthday is here and summer's pyre is set aflame. There is no defeat in this; rather, it is a bonfire to welcome winter.

I have often said that of the seasons in our section I like best spring and autumn. Spring brings a renewal of ancient enchantment. I am always astonished by the first flower, the slow greening of the bough. And autumn combines the best of summer—the mellow sunshine, the clear air—and the cool nights of spring.

Perhaps young people prefer summer. But during those months occur a great many things I happen not to like—the leaves grow dusty, the rain is withheld, the brook runs dry. As August comes in, the spring flowers, which were in such superb profusion, have gone and the summer roses are brown against the walls. And when we carry trays to the terrace for evening supper we are always aware of the malicious mosquito and the horrid little gnat, to say nothing of the spiteful black fly.

In summer, housework is something of a chore. We lighten it in every possible way but there are always days when we stagger reluctantly about our work. And when I look from the windows and don't see the Sound, I know that summer mist and humidity are upon us. But in October I rise with a new vitality and even housecleaning is not a distasteful idea.

Do you like to throw things away? Well, not always throw them, but discard them or give them to someone who can use them? For a person with a passion for collecting, I am also devoted to uncollecting. Often I save things only to look at them in a sort of fury and "unsave" them at once.

My children are hoarders. Even now we are begging the last one who is near home to clear out desk and bureau drawers. We thought we did it—with his permission—when we moved, but there is still a fearsome accumulation. I sometimes think my descendants have kept every matchbook, gadget, and postcard which has ever come their way.

I have a fairly tidy mind. There are, I admit, some letters I have held onto, but the number grows less each year. I have never kept clippings, except certain special ones, like the magazine record of our trip Down Under. I did keep a lot of paper work relative to the writing I did for various government and other organizations during World War II. They sat fatly in my files, all these things, and I was in two minds about them. But my daughter-in-law came to my rescue. I discovered that she was keeping scrapbooks about me, one personal, one impersonal. With joy I proceeded to dump into her lap, via the mails, all the things relating to my work, to family, and to other matters which I couldn't bear to destroy yet didn't really want to keep.

Take my mail, which is heavy. Sometimes letters come to me from strangers, letters so kind that I wish to keep them. But my other self steps in and the growing accumulation starts to haunt my slumbers. My regular mail is destroyed as soon as it is answered. I have in my study no less than three scrapbaskets. One is a sturdy bushel basket, another is a taller but thinner object, and the third is of metal and has written across it in gold letters the startling words "Faith's Rubbish."

These baskets, together with all those in the other rooms, seem to be perpetually full. I always rejoice, Tuesdays and Fridays, when the trashman comes around and I empty all the baskets into the biggest one of all, which sits on the back porch.

I wish that I might as easily discard the continuing false thinking, the carried-over prejudices, the dusty intolerances, the habits and errors which are, of course, the accumulation of years. It would be wonderful to tear these up and throw them away, most appropriately depositing them in the metal container labeled "Faith's Rubbish." For if there is one thing I've learned it is that we all carry about with us a tremendous burden of rubbish. You can name it as well as I—the regrets, the ifs and might-have-beens, as well as the clinging to old, outworn things never really good for us.

Sometimes I wake up at night cold with terror, hot with shame, thinking of my thousand and one sins of omission. Somehow they seem worse than the sins committed, because a great many things we do hurt only ourselves—not all of them, of course, but many—and the things we have left undone have hurt multitudes.

Still, to sit down and brood about these matters does us no good; brooding does no one any good. All we can do is pick up and go on, doing the best we can. And, of course, to find peace we must make it, not only with others but with ourselves.

During the autumn I have a chance to observe Nature's housekeeping. She goes on with her throwing-away all year. She is an untidy housekeeper. She uses a vast, brutal broom of wind, she uses rain and snow and ice. And so, particularly in spring and autumn, the dead boughs snap and fall, the twig is discarded. Soon now the glowing leaves, the glorious color, will be in drifts of gold and scarlet, mauve and rose, on grass and roadway. They will clog the gutters of the roofs, and householders will ascend on ladders to clear them out. The brooks and ponds will be choked with them, and they will float downstream, a deep-piled colored carpet, and wither and dry. And those which are not burned by man will quietly rot and enrich the earth.

Nature has a way of helping us to find the peace that is always there, waiting, within each of us. My last holiday was short, but I was able to sleep in the salt air, walk in the sun, and watch the waves roll in from Spain, in a very quiet place on Cape Cod after the majority of the summer visitors had gone. This is a section I knew first in my very young childhood, again when I was in my twenties, and then did not rediscover until a few years ago. I have never been able to make up my mind in which surroundings the greatest peace is imparted to the vulnerable spirit. I have felt peace high among the mountains, and again by the sea; I have felt it on the sea in a ship, and in a Hawaiian valley. I have experienced it when the snow lay deep at the top of a ski run, and on a New England farm in autumn. I have felt it in the quiet of my own patch of land at sunup or eventide, and in the still of my own room, waking at night. I cannot truthfully say that I have ever captured it in a city street, and yet I suppose it must be there. For reason tells me that the surroundings do not as much impart as contribute, that the peace you know originates within yourself; that the setting in which you recognize it is just a key turning.

I have always been too susceptible to surroundings and deplore it, feeling that something must be lacking if I am more at ease in my heart in one place than in another. Possibly for this reason I have been subjected to considerable necessary discipline. I have never liked a city for living, yet have lived in cities much of my life. I've always dreaded hospitals, the sights and odors, the implications, the sense of weariness and grief, of pain and never-ending battle that hangs over them. And yet I have spent a great deal of time in hospitals, rarely as a patient (when you are a patient your attitude changes) but often as a visitor.

I count myself more fortunate than most in that for some years I have lived in pleasant places and have been able fully to indulge my mania for birds, my unwearying passion for sunrise and sunset and for the moon afloat in a dark sky—a silver sliver or rising full and golden—my love for the sound of water running free, the benison of trees, the shift of seasons. In the country, even only a little distance away from the arteries leading to the towns, rain seems to fall more graciously and snow is so much whiter.

To me, the wheel of the seasons is a great happening. I never tire of it. Sitting at our east window, looking down past the trees, in such heavy foliage this year, to the pond, I see daily miracles—bird and animal, leaf and fruit. For over a year now I have watched and soon there will be no leaves.

But I do not think that the fallen leaf is a saddening thing. When the trees are bare, the view is clearer. When the familiar birds have departed on their mysterious migrations, the stranger birds will come, bright as dreams, staying a moment, finding food and shelter, and going on again.

And so while the torch burns along the branch and trembles in the leaf and this little place flames up in courage, before the gray days and the white hush set in, many happy returns of my birthday to you—and, if it be designated, to me.

NOVEMBER

1. ✿ *No Road Is Straight*

When in the summer of 1936 we moved to the country, I said to myself, "This is it. Here I shall live and die. This is for keeps."

I have often said that nothing on earth would induce me to return to a city to live. I could not even imagine such a thing; also, I would never be faced with making this decision. But the road is never straight, and if a decision means the happiness and peace of mind of someone dearer to you than yourself—why, then, it's taken before you know it and without a regret.

I believe that regret is one of the most miserable

burdens we are compelled, at one time or another, to carry. In recent months Regret has been my constant companion. Her face is as familiar to me as my own. She walked beside me daily. She sat at table with me, and at night lay down with me so that I could not sleep. I have often met Regret but never before has she been my guest for as long a period of time.

It is, of course, futile and foolish to regret something that you cannot now remedy. The burdens of regret or guilt are, however, not to be dismissed lightly, no matter how often you tell yourself that these are burdens to be discarded, laid down, forgotten. If you are then to go on usefully, you cannot do it, at least not for more than a little while at a time. I sometimes think that the bitterest tears are shed not in the company of grief but in that of regret, which is, I suppose, a form of grief. To wake in that black night and go over the same old ground, saying, "If I had not done this," or "If I had done that . . ." To lie in darkness, retracing every step of the way, and recognizing years too late, the wrong signpost, the fatal turn, is almost beyond endurance. But somehow you battle it out and learn, step by step, to forgive yourself; if you are fortunate, you will be given a second chance.

I have just passed another birthday and tell myself hopefully that there is yet time—time in which to make up for the bygone errors, time to erase the mistakes, time in which to be happy. For a birthday always seems to me the start of a personal new year. Everyone celebrates January 1, a holiday that is common to all. But your own birthday is something special. You are revived and regenerated, whether it be your tenth or twentieth, your sixtieth or eightieth birthday.

An autumn birthday seems most appropriate. There is yet time before winter closes in—though winter is beautiful, too. What a time is autumn! It is filled with light and color, with deep-blue skies, blazing stars, and in one part of the world, with such a magnificence of gold and ruby, scarlet and grape, yellow and bronze, that the heart almost stops at the contemplation of it.

The tender uncertainty, the reluctant bloom, the fresh renewal of spring have gone. Gone, too, are the lush green ways of summer, the heavy heat, the brooding storms, the lavish spilling forth of sunshine, of quiet rain, and of flowers. In their place we have the mellow warm days, the cool sweet nights. To drive through, or walk in, the woods is unforgettable, or to sit out of doors and watch the red moon rise and hear the wind come rushing through the branches. As the days grow shorter they become more measurable, and every minute is packed with wonder and excitement. In autumn there is no time to waste.

Each year that I live brings me closer to the knowledge of the power and the glory. When you are young, so much is taken for granted—the bird on the wing, the flower in the grass, the sleepy song of brooks, the changing skies. These and more—a friend's smile, the touch of a beloved hand, children laughing at their play, a dusty dog running home along a dusty road. The simple things, and many that are not so simple. But when you grow into maturity, into age, nothing can be taken for granted. Each day must be lived completely and none wasted. The brilliant leaf is one of millions, but each holds the power and the glory, and must so be contemplated.

I recently spoke of the terrible moment that comes to many people when prayer seems impossible. Yet looking from a window, whether in country or in city, I am sure that the entire world lifts its heart in prayer—even if it is not always aware of it. In the still byways of the country, prayer is often unconscious—a silent offering of gratitude. In the busy streets, elbow to elbow with strangers who share your common mortality, who suffer and hope, who rejoice and struggle, prayer rises higher than the tallest building. Consciously or unconsciously man, in his humble insignificance, must worship, must recognize his gratitude, must lean. He is compelled to ask for help from his intolerable burden, or he will perish.

When, not so long ago, I found that I dared not pray for myself, I came to such an empty place in my daily living that it was unendurable. No matter what had ever happened to me before I had always been able to find the one great solace. To lose it now seemed the worst thing that had ever come to me in my whole life. But there was a way, and a very simple one. One can cease wishing to pray for yourself, for anyone, for anything. One can just say: "I've done what I could, Father. So now it is in Your Hands." I believe from the depths of my being that this is an unfailing prayer. Somehow, things must come right, for all involved.

If regret is the heaviest burden, despair is the most cynical. It is, I think, a form of sin. Having despaired, I look back with incredulity and shame. I am not ashamed of regret, but to have despaired is a dreadful thing. In God's plan there is no blueprint for despair. For if we despair we do not trust. If we do not trust we do not believe, and if belief has been cast aside, there is no meaning in having lived.

When Jesus bade those who were heavy-laden, those who were weary, to come unto Him, He meant exactly that. Those of us who *have* come, after the most appalling struggle, know how true the words, how valid the promise, how great the reward. Has He not said, "I will give you rest"?

Rest from the burden, the doubt, the despair, rest from the struggle, the problem, the wretched business of losing one's way, not knowing where the road goes, what the turn will bring, not seeing one inch beyond the blind personal darkness. When the burden is laid down, and the belief spoken, the trust renewed, the skies are light again and the road is clear once more. It has never been straight, you know. You look ahead and see the miles that are the years before you, but for only a little way.

You must travel step by step, always trusting, knowing that this is your road and that when the going is rough it will soon be made smooth and that when the night falls the brighter day must dawn.

It has often been said that only a hair's breadth separates love from hate. I don't think I believe this. But I am certain that there is a narrow margin between trust and doubt, happiness and despair. The margin is the little space in which you linger, as the road turns, fearful of going ahead, yet knowing you cannot go back. The steps you have taken to this turn were taken in your doubt and your despair, and you wonder, with utmost weariness, how long they must continue beyond the bend. But it is beyond the bend that the good things lie—the trust and the happiness.

I wish for you a wonderful November—clear skies and friends, work and play, and all you most love near to you. I wish for you the road that, while it may turn when least you expect it, will lead you into light and joy.

And now—

If you have remained with me this long, I do thank you, very much.

You will have disagreed or agreed, as the case may be; you will have been bored or indifferent or interested, perhaps even a little angry (which I would prefer to the bored or indifferent). Whatever you have thought or felt while reading this small book, I hope you have thought and felt *something*.

Physical growth is a slow process; mental and emotional maturing is even slower; but the most gradual development in man is that of his spiritual nature. We know few people of whom we can say that the development is complete.

In every age, era, and generation men have sought for something which, while beyond themselves, is also a part of themselves. They will continue to do so. There will be many more miracles of science—the age of the push button, of the prolongation of life upon this plane of existence—and men will learn that a discovery which can destroy this little world can also save it, for there are two sides to every coin. But as long as Earth spins upon her axis there will be immutable values: the search after God; the search for the meaning of man's essential spiritual life; the choice between good and evil.

Long before Christianity, men worshiped, and

looked for God within themselves. For the imperative needs have always existed and always will exist: the need for God, by whatever name you call Him; the need for spiritual nourishment, a hunger and thirst as demanding as those of the body; the need for Love.

All love is a part of God, as a spark is a part of the Divine Fire.

We shall be judged, I think, by the love we have offered, given, and shared: the personal love of family, friend, and neighbor; the impersonal love that is service; the love we cannot quite put into words, not even in prayer, that is the love of God. . . .